SIMONE

Volume II

TAJ SHAMARI

CONTENTS

PROLOGUE

NAYELI

I JUST DROPPED Simone back to our apartment and was now headed back to Jessie's.

Me: I'm on the way.

Headache: Ok, baby. You still mad?

I tossed it off to the side. My head was swarming. There were two babies growing inside of me. Two humans at the same time. Twins. Gemini. Thinking back, I didn't know how that fact went over my head. He was a twin, his mom was a twin, and for God's sake, it was all in the name.

And what about my plans? I'd have to put my restaurant on hold for who knows how long. Caring for two newborns, I'd probably never make it back to following my dreams. My life would be all about them now. That was how it happened for my mom and her mom. I wanted to be able to follow through with my career plans before I brought children into my world.

God, my mom, I thought. She was gonna flip. Oddly enough, she was the stricter parent, and she hadn't even met Jessie yet. I mentioned him before, but briefly. I didn't want her to know how fast we'd been moving; she was a traditional woman, and she expected that of me as well. Not only was I going to be bringing a new man around, not even three months after Cameron, but on top of that, I was already pregnant and with twins. Thankfully, I'd have my dad there to cause some type of interference with my mom, but that wouldn't last through the supernatural portion of the conversation because, after all these years, he still had no clue of that side of my mom. A lone tear fell from my eye as I rode the remainder of the distance in silence.

As soon as I walked in, I heard him on the game, which had to be the most annoying invention ever. Upon coming into his view, he paused it, tossing the controller aside. I went to sit beside him on the couch, kicking out of my slides. He pulled my feet up into his lap as I lay my head back on the arm of the couch.

"So?" he asked as I rolled my eyes because he'd already known.

I sat up, looking over to him with narrowed eyes before handing him the ultrasound. "What are we going to do, Jessie?" I asked seriously.

He pulled me closer to him. "Baby, chill. I got us forever. We have time before they get here to find a new spot. I'ma keep doing what I'm doing, and you're going to pick a location for your restaurant to give you something to do. You're not going to stress my babies out. You're going to finish school, we'll have some more babies, and live happily ever after," he finished before kissing me. He pulled away, wiping my tears.

"Your grandma showed you all that, too?" I asked sarcastically as he burst into laughter before kissing me and pulling me into his lap. I loved that although he always wanted to be so controlling, he took my career into consideration for our future together. Thankfully, he didn't expect me to be a housewife. He supported my career, and I loved that about him.

I guess I automatically figured my dreams would be put on hold because, traditionally, that was how it usually went when children were brought into the mix. Thankfully, I didn't have the kind of man that expected that of me. This whole relationship was all still pretty new. At least, for me.

"Nah, for real, baby, we good. We're gonna always be good. You need to know that." He was so cute. Between the curse and the shit he said to me, it was hard to stay mad. He kissed my stomach, smiling. "I'm finna be a daddy, though." He wrapped his big arms tightly around me, leaving light butterfly kisses around my neck. I smiled after taking a deep breath. At least I had Simone to go through this with. It was crazy how we both turned out to be pregnant at the same time. That curse had done a number on us.

I found instant comfort in the fact that we would be going through this together. Our kids would grow up together just as we had. They would be only a few months apart just as we were and were already destined to be best friends for life as well. Nothing happening in our lives right now was what we planned or anything we could have ever imagined. We were on a road to being a chef and chemistry teacher. Those were our concrete plans ever since ninth grade. This supernatural life was nowhere in sight until recently and had come in and rearranged a lot. Not so much as my career for me, but my personal life. Simone, on the other hand, was more interested in the chemistry of her magic these days.

Suddenly, my head was screaming in distress.

"Simone!" I whispered as a nerve wrecking chill ran through my body, and I wiggled out of his hold in search of my phone. My whole body was in distress and covered in chills. *What the fuck is going on?*

I called Simone's phone countless times to no avail. Panicking, I hurriedly dialed Nathan and waited impatiently for him to pick up. As soon as I heard the receiver, I spoke. "Nathan, where is Simone? What happened?" I asked frantically. I knew something was wrong. I could feel it. I'd never felt this before.

"Man, I don't know. She was telling me she was pregnant, then she disappeared. I can't find her ass anywhere. Nayeli, what y'all been up to?" he asked me skeptically. My eyebrows scrunched. He continued. "That lil' Boston trip was a cover up for her to go to Salem. She thinks her dad is still alive." How hadn't I known any of this? How was she able to keep that from me when we were connected? I was supposed to be able to sense everything with her, but I guess I couldn't read her mind. I thought I'd at least be able to sense her apprehension. I hoped all this sneaking around didn't become a habit. He paused briefly. "Nayeli, you think they got my baby?"

I sat on the other end stunned. I didn't know what to think about that shit. Everything that had been done her whole life was to prevent that very thing from happening. If that was the case, though, all hell was going to break loose in little ole Mobile, Alabama.

CHAPTER 1

NATHAN

I REPEATEDLY POUNDED on the steering wheel, trying to let out some of this frustration as I sped down the interstate. I was about to meet Nayeli, Eva, and my mom at her salon. This shit was really fuckin' with me. I needed to know where she was, and I needed to know now. Ever since the day I walked into her life, I was supposed to keep her safe, and I failed. After all this time, I fuckin failed.

"Fuck!" I yelled as my phone dinged.

JC: Yo, you good, bro? What you need me to do?

I was sick. I didn't even know yet. He wasn't coming along with Nayeli because this wasn't the time for introductions. All that shit could be done once I had my arms around my girl. My nigga and I were supposed to be celebrating becoming dad's and talking shit over the fact that we were gonna be experiencing it at the same time. I was supposed to be kissing and cuddling with my girl right now while we discussed how we were going to be as parents. Whoever was responsible for this was sure to feel me before this was all over. I'd been able to contain my calmness through so much bullshit, but fuckin' with my family was the best and quickest way to meet the *fuck it* side of me.

That part of me didn't care about shit or nobody else in my way. I hated to become that nigga, but at this rate, I didn't see any other way. Whoever was responsible was fuckin' with my future and the future of my family. Sometimes, I wished I never met Simone, simply because she was a weak spot for me. My biggest weak spot. Before her, it was just me and my mom; she always was able to more than protect herself. I ain't give a fuck about nobody else, so a motherfucka couldn't really get to me.

I felt like I was out of my car before I even cut it off. I burst through the door to find my mom and Nayeli, who were both already in Mobile. Eva would be here soon. I paced the floor aimlessly. All I saw was red, and that was all I would see if anything happened to her or my baby.

Eva burst in, locking the door behind her. "What happened?" She looked to everyone in the room as I explained to them how she disappeared right in front of me.

"I went by the cabin, but I couldn't see anything." I looked at Eva and Nayeli. "Can either of you see it because of the blood tie?" I was sure that wasn't where she was, though. This wasn't of her own doing. She was taken. I was sure of it, and I was desperate to find any leads.

My mom looked confused. "No, it doesn't work like that. I'll explain later." She directed the last part to my mom, who still looked puzzled. "Why would she have gone there so abruptly? The way you made it seem I don't think this is something she did willingly. We need to weigh our other options," she said skeptically, obviously thinking the worst, as I already had.

I was losing it internally. I was trying hard to hold in how I was really feeling because I wasn't in the mood to be scolded. Right now, I wanted to tear some shit up!

"We need to visit Gabby. I know you can use your connection to her for that, so we won't need the necklace," I said as she nodded before grabbing up the candles and closing the blinds to the salon. "I know that will work," I repeated to myself. It had to. I needed to see her mom so she could tell us where to look for Simone's dad's family. I was short on ideas, and there was no doubt in my mind they or her grandma alone were the culprits.

We sat in a circle, holding hands and chanting, using Eva as our anchor. We were lifted from the ground before returning to our previous spots.

Once in the cabin, Nayeli and I hurriedly jumped up in search of Gabby. Eva and Tally stood in shock. This wasn't going to be an easy visit by a long shot. The two hadn't laid eyes on their best friend in twenty-one years, and even crazier, she was still that same girl from twenty-one years ago. I actually wasn't sure why neither of them had been over to visit with her yet when Nayeli and I had, but that was a concern for another day. Today, it was about Simone and our baby.

We searched every inch of the cabin, and she was nowhere in sight.

"What the fuck?" I yelled in frustration as my mom's head swung in my direction swiftly, eyes chastising me. "I'm sorry, Ma, but how she ain't here? She can't even leave."

Suddenly, the screen door swung open as Gabby entered, her hair pulled back into a loose ponytail and sporting a small tank top covered by a pair of dirty overalls. She was carrying a basket of fruits and vegetables. She looked up at me startled.

"Oh, hey, baby. What are you doing he..." Her words trailed off as everyone else came into view. The room filled with silence as the threesome took in each other. There were no words, only misty eyes. "E.. e... Tal..." she tried to say as her words caught in her throat.

She ran full speed into them, pulling them into a hug. One that each of them needed. The room filled with ugly cries as I stood back waiting on them to finish their moment, impatiently. It was inevitable. They'd been missing each other all these years. Neither of the three had been in communication. At least, for the first eight

years for my mom and Eva. After finding Simone, the two recon-
nected secretly as they both played the background.

She pulled away as her eyes scanned the room before looking
back at me for answers.

"Where's my baby?" she asked, taking in everyone's demeanor as
the previous mist reappeared. "Nathan?"

"One minute, we were talking. The next, she was gone. She just
disappeared right in front of me." I cleared the emotion from my
voice. "She got in her head that her dad is still alive and that little
Boston trip she planned was a coverup to sneak off to Salem to look
for him."

"Salem!" Gabby exclaimed as everyone else's eyes bucked in
shock. "This girl is going to drive me crazy." She sighed, taking a
seat on the couch. "Salem? Really?"

Tally and Eva snickered. "You got some nerve. You were more
than two handfuls. She's got it honest," Tally said as Eva remained
silent. She hugged her and shed a couple of tears, but she hadn't
said anything to her.

I stepped up. "Yo, we can get into all that after I lay eyes on my
girl," I informed them seriously. "Now, her grandma... where can I
find her?" I asked Gabby.

"I understand your frustration, but that is a suicide mission if
taken without thought-out planning. It's too risky. We can't help
her if we're compromised."

"Y'all don't understand," I yelled. "She's pregnant. I need eyes
on her now!"

Everyone stood around in shock. Speechless. I sat back on the
couch looking at Nayeli, whose eyes were bucked, pleading for me
not to mention her, but that wasn't my business to tell.

I pulled the ultrasound from my pocket and leaned forward,
staring down at it. I couldn't take this shit out on them. We were all
in the same boat. Gabby sat beside me, looking at the ultrasound,
smiling. "If they hadn't changed anything, they should be right in
the center of Downtown Mobile. The coven owns a restaurant

called *The Cottage*. There is a hidden door underneath the floorboard in the kitchen near the stove, but you're still gonna need a plan."

Gabby took the ultrasound from my hands and smiled down at it brightly before her eyebrows dropped in confusion. "Wait. If Simone isn't with y'all, then how did y'all get here?"

We all knew you had to have a special possession of the deceased to visit, and that possession for Gabby was her necklace.

"We are using Eva as an anchor right now because of your guy's familial connection," Tally informed as Gabby and Eva briefly locked eyes. There was clear tension between them. I looked away, thinking. I needed to get some of the other coven members together. I stilled.

"What if this has something to do with whatever happened to Jada? She has been missing for about two months," I thought aloud, making me heat up again. I put the picture back into my pocket before standing. "I ain't wasting no more time. Y'all ready?" I asked, looking at everyone.

"Be careful, Nathan!" Gabby said to me. "And you two should come back and see me," she said to Eva and my mom. Eva scoffed as we all joined hands before appearing back in the hair salon. She was clearly angry about something, but once again, that was a concern for another day.

I quickly stood, pulling my phone and rounding everyone up via text. The plan was to disable anyone who stood in our way, but I saw blood. I wanted blood. I felt tested and had a point to prove, so everyone knew not to ever test me this way ever again. We were all going to meet here and move that way soon after they arrived. I just hoped it wasn't too late. I tried not to think that way because I was going to fuck some shit up if it was!

CHAPTER 2

SIMONE

I'D BEEN STANDING and sitting in total darkness for I didn't know how long. I had no idea where I was, and upon appearing in the mysterious place, my hands were immediately bound by rope, which also had to be bound by some type of spell because I couldn't get it off, and I couldn't use my magic. I had no idea who was responsible, but my money was on dear old granny. There wasn't anybody else out there that could possibly have a problem with me. For the most part, I stayed to myself. Except for that bitch, Jada, but she didn't have the balls. She was one of those *start shit but can't finish it* type of bitches, so Granny was my definite answer. How she found me was what I was waiting to understand.

More time had gone by. Something about total darkness made time seem longer. I was annoyed with myself that the one time I needed my phone it wasn't glued to my hand as usual.

I sighed thinking of Nathan and Nayeli, who were both probably losing it. Nayeli was probably holding it together a hundred times better than Nathan. I just told him I was pregnant, and he wasn't even able to react properly before I was whisked away by some unknown assailant.

Suddenly, the room was filled with rows of some of the brightest lights I'd ever seen in my life, blinding me. My eyes were closed tightly as I heard the distant clicks of stilettos against the hard floor. My vision was taking its dearest time to adjust. They drew closer and closer before stopping in front of me, then they circled me as my eyes focused.

I squinted, and disgust-filled eyes looked back at me. "So, you're what all the fuss has been about?" She scoffed, flipping her bouncy, blonde hair to the other side. She wore a white blouse tucked into a navy-blue pinstripe skirt, accompanied by what I assumed to be red bottoms. She didn't seem like the type of woman to wear anything that wasn't designer.

"In the flesh," I replied, standing and looking around what seemed to be a storage room as I took notice of the stacks of boxes, tables, and chairs pushed along the walls, as if they had been moved to make room.

I wasn't afraid. This day was sure to come sooner or later. I couldn't hide forever, and I didn't want to. No, I wasn't afraid, I was angry. It coursed through me rapidly for many reasons. At the moment, the main reason being she'd interrupted me and my man's moment of finding out we'd created a life together. She wasn't going to do to me what she'd done to my mom.

I wanted to lay eyes on who was responsible for my life going the way it had. All the obstacles that could have been avoided. I was also starting to wonder who the real threat was to whom. There couldn't have been this much hate in the world. Or maybe there could've been because I despised her, and I didn't even know her. Everything I heard of her over the short time I'd known the truth of my life had been evil. She didn't know me and didn't feel the need to get to know me. She only saw me as a problem that needed solving, and in turn, I saw her as the same. She'd been the biggest problem in my life since birth, and this problem would have to get dealt with soon. Now, here we were. In the middle of a standoff.

"What am I doing here? I've got shit to do, Granny!"

Her disgust deepened. "I guess I could see why Jada wanted to get rid of you." I quickly gazed in her direction. "You're an entitled little shit. I won't feel anything about getting rid of you."

I scoffed. "Is that what happened? Bitch came down here and gave me up then ran off until you took care of her problem. Did I get everything right?"

I guess she did have some balls, but they weren't big enough for her to deal with me herself. I hated a scary bitch. If I made it out of this, she was going to see me.

"All except one minor detail." She smiled. "I appreciated the information of the problem still out there, but I didn't like the boldness of the little black bitch. She's dead. Just as dead as your dear old mom. Just as dead as you're about to be. By the time I'm done, your kind will learn and know your place in my city," she ended with a chuckle as rage took over me.

I ran at her full speed, hands still bound. I was flung backward, hitting a stack of chairs before being restrained against the wall as she neared.

"Did I strike a nerve?" she asked sarcastically, displaying a faux sad face. I winced as a sharp pain shot through my back, unable to move before hyperventilating, trying to catch the wind that was just knocked from me.

She started in my direction. "That bitch you call mom is responsible for everything that went wrong with my family. Poisoning my bloodline with her filthy blood. I can't lie, though, the little bitch was smart. I'd give her that because there was no way you were supposed to survive. Then being hidden for so long... Bravo, Gabrielle Dupree." She clapped.

I smirked. "Do you think you'll get away with this? Chasity finds out about this, and you'll lose her forever, Granny Cheryl. You'll do anything for the two of them, right? How can you hate your own granddaughter so much?" I asked. I had to know.

She stared in confusion. "How do you know of my daughter?"

I smirked. "My aunt and I spend plenty of time together."

She scoffed. "She's not going to find out about anything, and you're nothing of mine. Nothing to me but a nuisance. Another little black bitch plaguing my city. I know about the curse on you little whorish girls. Any male in this city could be your dad."

"Yeah, that's why I have visions of conversations my dad had with you. About you. You know, he really hated you. I definitely see why. Must suck, though, having the only two children you have in this world despise your presence. I don't even feel that way about my mom, and I've only known her for a couple of months."

She quickly advanced. "What do you mean you've *known her*? Where is she?"

I smiled. "Now, that's none of your concern, is it?" I asked as my eyebrows gathered in the middle of my forehead.

Her hand instantly wrapped around my neck as she squeezed. "I'm sorry, can you repeat that?" she asked with a devious grin as she placed her ear in front of me. I continued to struggle for air. "I can't hear you, granddaughter. Where are all those slick words now?" she asked before releasing me as I gasped for air. "I'm going to enjoy this." She turned to walk off, releasing me from the wall as my hands remained bound.

She stopped, turning back in my direction as I keeled over, still gasping for air. "By chance, would you mind telling me what you were doing on my property in Massachusetts?" she inquired.

I looked up to her. I'd known she hadn't sold that cabin, so my suspicions must have been true. Was I just steps away from my dad back then? Would I ever get to see him if she were to successfully carry out whatever she had in store for me?

She cleared her throat, rushing my response, as if she hadn't just choked the shit out of me. "Looking for my dad. I know he's in there."

She stood shocked briefly before smiling. "Too bad you're never going to find out now isn't—"

"Mother, what on Earth are you doing?" Chasity's voice startled the both of us. I hurriedly looked up, feeling instant relief. "Simone, are you okay?" she asked me from across the medium sized room. I nodded before she turned her attention back to Cheryl. "Why the fuck are you doing this? What is your purpose? She's part of Chase, and you're trying to hurt her. Really? This is your granddaughter," she tried to reason.

I stood back, watching the exchange, secretly fearing for my baby. Just hours ago, I was distraught about the very thought of having a baby right now. Now that Cheryl had restricted the air in my body and manhandled me, I hoped whatever Nathan and I created was stronger than the both of us combined because I didn't want anything to happen to my baby. Nathan seemed so happy before I was snatched away.

Poor Nathan. My protector. He was probably losing his shit right now. Still not feeling a sense of time, I could only assume that hours had gone by, and he hadn't been able to locate me, which only meant whatever Cheryl had done to me was blocking it. She probably made it seem like I'd fallen off the face of the Earth. She'd done the same to my dad when I tried locator spells on him.

My poor babies. I'd heard what distress could do to a growing fetus, and I was only two months along. Poor Nathan because now he not only had me to protect, but an impending baby, and he couldn't lay eyes on my right now.

I needed for this whole nightmare of a day to be over soon!

CHAPTER 3

CHASITY

THE CURRENT STANDOFF between my mom and I was sure to end in one of our demises. Preferably hers. She'd more than crossed the line, and she was sure to find out just how far over that line she'd gone this time.

For as long as I could remember, she'd been extremely racist, for what reason, neither Chase nor myself knew. After all these years, she was holding on tight to her hateful agenda. Her life had to be in constant misery. She left no room for happiness. I don't think I'd ever seen her happy. Just evil at all times, and the rest of the coven blindly followed behind her. She was supposed to have been the most powerful of our coven, but as quiet as it's kept, she wasn't.

At very young ages, both Chase and I surpassed her power. Thank God for my dad's blood also coursing through our veins. The good in him outweighed the evil in her, otherwise, there was no telling how my brother and I would have turned out. I hated to think about it, but sometimes, I wished we could switch out the parent we lost. The world would be a better place if my dad were here, and my mom weren't.

I looked over to Simone standing back in the corner rubbing her neck.

"What did she do to you, Simone?" I asked, fuming. This woman was un-fucking-believable.

"She choked me," Simone forced out just as I balled my fist, and my mom's breathing was now restricted as she gasped repeatedly.

"Doesn't feel too good, huh, Cheryl?" I asked her rhetorically as she dropped to her knees, and I opened my hand. "Oh no, you don't get to go that easily. By the way, I went to visit that cabin. Remember, the one you *sold* after dad died? Yeah, that one," I confirmed as her eyes ballooned. "Found something pretty interesting behind a little wall."

She looked up to me, and for the first time in my life, I saw fear cross her features. "You don't understand, Chasity."

"Your time for talking is up, Cheryl," I interrupted. She didn't have anything to say that anybody wanted to hear. "You don't understand. You enjoy toying with other's lives. We'll see how you like it."

I heard footsteps approaching. I didn't need to be on guard. I knew exactly who they belonged to. My suspicions were confirmed as shock covered both Simone and my mom's face. Cheryl was speechless and fucked. Definitely fucked! The wrath she was going to feel behind this was the last thing she'd expected.

He walked past me, looked past Cheryl, not even acknowledging her presence, and he zeroed in on Simone, who wore the exact same expression. With the flick of his finger, the ropes bounding her hands unraveled and fell to the floor. She rubbed out her wrist as he drew closer to her. His hand went up to caress her cheek as a single tear fell from her eye. He wiped it away, cupping her face between the palm of both hands, staring at her lovingly.

"You look just like her," he expressed, smiling as she returned one. "You know who I am, right?" he asked as his eyebrows dropped before she nodded, and he chuckled lightly.

She stared at him lovingly as well, and I wept for the little girl who wasn't given a chance to be a daddy's girl. As well as for my brother, who was robbed of the chance to become a girl dad. He would've been great at parenting.

"I can't believe you are a grown woman now, last I saw you, you fit snugly in my arms," he reminisced before more tears fell from her eyes, and he pulled her into a tight hug. She bawled into his chest before wincing. He pulled away to look her over as he got a glimpse of the red marks on her neck. I could see his demeanor change from behind him. Chase was a sweetheart, but this was his daughter, whom he was seeing for the first time in twenty-one years, and she was being tortured by his mom. Everybody had a button, and this was her second attempt on Simone's life. The first one, she'd put him under a sleep spell for twenty-one years. That button was broken!

"Who did this?" I heard him ask. It was low and threatening. Simone looked past him into Cheryl's eyes. He turned in our direction, and anger consumed him. Besides the long wild hair and long beard, he didn't look too different from before.

I couldn't believe my mom would stoop this low to fulfill her hatred. Taking my twin away from me for so long, making me think he was dead, and taking Simone's dad away for her whole life. He bore into her. "When I get my strength back, I'm going to tear you to pieces. You've terrorized enough and don't deserve to live much longer."

Hurt crossed her features. The audacity. She was comical. "Chase, I'm your mother."

"You ain't shit to me, Cheryl. This is my daughter," he said, pointing back at Simone and taking short steps toward us. "And how old is she? Where the fuck is my fiancée?" he asked rhetorically, taking more steps. "And where the fuck have I been for twenty one years of my daughter's life? You're dead!"

His anger toward her had long surpassed mine. She pushed him too far years ago, when she first threatened Gabrielle's life. Not even trying to take into account that her son was in love with this woman or how he would feel if something happened to her. She claimed to love her children but didn't care about the things we cared about. She expected everyone to agree with whatever she felt, but she didn't get that from us. We had our own minds, and she hated it and constantly tried to change it.

She launched toward the wall to ring the distress alarm and yelled out for the coven members. She stripped Simone of her magic for however long, and Chase was too weak to use his. He'd literally been asleep for twenty-one years in that fuckin cabin, so he was no help right now. We were outnumbered.

"I'll take care of her," I said as I snapped my fingers, sending them to Gabby's secret cabin.

I threw sleeping powder into Cheryl's face and caught her before jumping to a secret location I'd been working on just for her. I lay her down on the floor as I snatched up the keys to unlock the cell and placed her inside on top of the cot before I locked it.

I sat back in the chair across from her, thinking. I couldn't believe I had my brother back. It was still so surreal. Seeing him asleep in that bed took my breath away. He looked so peaceful. All this time he was here.

I'd known there was a reason I wasn't able to properly grieve his death. Because he had never died. Had it not been for Simone, I still wouldn't know anything. I wasn't expecting to actually find him there. I was just following Simone's hunch and thought if anything didn't turn up, at least I'd get to experience a bit of nostalgia.

I looked back over to my sleeping mom. The powder should have been wearing off any minute now. She wasn't going to like this at all, but she had to know this all would circle back around one day. After being unconscious for about an hour, her sudden groaning cut through the silence.

She sat straight up on the cot, surveying her surroundings before standing, stumbling a bit. "Chasity Blanche, let me out of here this instant," she demanded upon deaf ears.

I stood from my post. "I find it very comical that you can

attempt to make demands in your predicament." Her eyes narrowed as she flicked a finger. Nothing. Again, nothing. She glared at me in shock. "Nice, right?" I asked. "I've been working on this place for years, especially for you. Your very own prison, Mom. How do you like it?"

"The other members will be looking for me soon. You can't possibly think you'll get away with this." She was so sure of herself.

"Actually, I'm pretty sure they're just as tired of your shit as me." I walked closer to her cell. "Look around. This is it. This is home for you now. If you're a good girl, you'll be able to move out to the bedroom, but you can definitely kiss civilization goodbye." I turned to leave before stopping in my tracks. "I do have a question, though." I paused. "What were your plans? To have him locked away asleep forever? He'd have been better off dead!"

She sighed. "It wasn't supposed to be this way. I tried erasing that black bitch from his memory. Then I would have woken him up for good." Rage filled her eyes. "But every time, they came right back. Every. Single. Time. I guess I know why now. That little offspring had still been lurking in the shadows. I have no idea how she was even able to survive that."

I was disgusted. All of this because she didn't like who my brother had fallen in love with. She'd rather see him indisposed than enjoying his life to the fullest. That was no mother. That was a dictator. Someone who craved control, which was why this was so much easier than I expected. She finally looked back over to me, breaking her distant stare.

"You'd better be glad this place is all I have planned for you. You'd better hope Chase is never able to find it. If he does, death and solitude will be the least of your fuckin worries," I finished as I walked out.

CHAPTER 4

NAYELI

WE WERE NOW BACK at the hair salon pacing and waiting impatiently. We moved on the Salem witches, and by the time we'd gotten there, the only thing we could find was a rope on the ground, which only made Nathan spiral worse. Between him and Jessie, I couldn't settle my feelings about this.

As much as I tried, I couldn't feel her. At all. From the day I came into my abilities, we'd been able to feel everything from each other. I'd gotten used to that. The only thing I was supposed to be able to do, I couldn't. Now, my best friend, my sister, was missing. Nowhere to be found. Not a trace or trail to follow. My phone chimed.

Headache: You aight, baby? What y'all doing?

He wanted to be here, and he was supposed to be here. He was a part of the coven, but when we were around each other, we were drawn to each other. His hands would be all over me, and I didn't feel like going over this with my mom right now. This wasn't the time at all.

Me: Yes, baby. We're still looking for her, and Nathan is losing it.

I looked over at him continuously doing locator spells to no avail. He'd exhausted all options, and nothing had turned up. This had for sure been an eventful day. *I need my sister back*, I thought as my memory took me away.

12 years ago

I ran around the playground freely, enjoying the short time we had for recess. This was my favorite part of the day besides going home. I hated school, the work, and the other kids, so I stayed to myself a lot.

After quickly crossing the monkey bars for the third time today, I was in search of my next stop. Swings! I thought as I ran full speed in their direction. Stopping in my tracks, I observed the scene playing out directly behind the swings. I looked at the teachers out here with us, who weren't paying attention at all. A group of about five kids stood around one little girl pushing her onto the ground. Every time she got up, they'd do it again as they stood around laughing. The girl was crying, and no one came to help. She stood, and again, she was on the ground. They were taking turns. I hated bullies.

I huffed, running full speed into the last girl who pushed her down. She flew a few inches off the ground and over the head of the girl who was being bullied. I reached down to help her up while looking over at the group.

"Shayla and Morgan, I don't know why y'all always trying to bully somebody. Want me to beat y'all up again? Y'all want some, too?" I asked, turning my attention to the other three girls. They walked away after Shayla had gotten back up off the ground.

I turned back to the other girl who stood in front of me with her head hung. Taking in her appearance, I noticed she was dressed in what looked to be too small hand-me-downs, and her hair was pulled back into a messy ponytail, but she was really pretty.

"Thank you! You didn't have to do that," she said, looking down at her feet.

I blew a raspberry. "That was nothing. They deserved it, anyway." I brushed off. "My name is Nayeli, by the way."

"That's really pretty. My name is Simone."

We continued to talk throughout recess and during lunch because we weren't in the same third grade class. After school, I ran into her again.

"Hey, you walk home, too?" I asked as she nodded. "Do you have to go straight home? My mommy makes the best snacks, and I have a lot of toys, and my mom can take you home afterward."

She looked in the other direction briefly before nodding and walking side by side en route to my house. I only lived two streets over, so we were there in no time. I dropped my backpack by the front door and kicked off my shoes, and so did Simone.

"Maaaaa!" I yelled.

"Kitchen!"

As we entered the kitchen, my mom turned in my direction with a confused expression on her face.

"This is my new friend, Simone, Mommy." She sat back in one of the chairs at the table staring at Simone. "Can she stay for snacks and to play?" I asked, bottom lip poked out. That was how I always got my way.

"Simone... when is your birthday?" my mom asked weirdly, stumbling over her words.

"June 11, 1998," Simone murmured. My mom's hand went up to cover her mouth.

"Where do you live?"

"A couple of streets over with my foster family," Simone replied with her head hung low as my mom's face scrunched up as if she would cry.

I grabbed Simone's hand. "Mommy, can we go play now?" I whined. She'd been acting weird since we walked in... staring and asking all these questions. I didn't want her to scare my new friend away.

"Yeah, yeah! Go ahead, and I'll bring the snacks up," she said, reaching for her phone and dialing quickly. We played in my room for a couple of hours before eating dinner. Today had ended up being a good one. I made a new friend, and she was really cool.

I wiped the tears away. From that day forward, we were inseparable friends, and by the end of the following week, we were deemed sisters forever.

"Where the fuck is my sister?" I yelled.

Anything that wasn't attached to anything had flown in the direction of my voice hitting the wall opposite of me. My eyes bucked as I did a three sixty around the room. Everyone else's expressions matched mine. *Did I do that? How did I do that?* I thought.

Suddenly, an overwhelming feeling of relief came over me.

"Simone!" I exclaimed, smiling as everyone continued to look at me like I was crazy. "I can feel her. I can feel Simone!"

"Where?" Nathan asked, rising from his seat.

"She's safe." I smiled. "Come on," I said, reaching my hands out for Nathan and my mom, who held Tally's hand. "The cabin," I whispered to him as he quickly jumped the four of us to the wooded area.

"Where are we?" Tally asked. "Why would she be out here?"

"Nathan," We heard Simone call out softly, appearing a couple of feet in front of us.

As soon as he laid eyes on her, he wasted no time running in her direction and picking her up. "You okay, baby? Is the baby okay?"

She sighed. "Yes, Nathan," she said, looking at the three of us as I gave her a look saying, *yup, he told everyone.*

"Baby, put me down," she requested as he completely ignored her. She rolled her eyes, holding her hands out. "Grab my hand," she said to Tally, who looked confused as well. Skeptically, they obliged as the cabin appeared before all of us.

"Wha... where? What?" Tally rambled. Nathan walked, and they followed suit. I pulled out my phone to text Jessie.

Me: Found her

"You're not the only one happy to see her, Nathan," I declared, rolling my eyes. He ignored me, continuously holding on to her as if scared she'd disappear again.

"This is where Gabby is on the ancestral plain," Tally blurted in realization, looking around the room.

Simone's gaze landed on her. "Y'all went to see my mom? How?"

Before she could answer, we heard a small noise alerting us all. My mom and Tally gasped as a man came into view.

"Chase?" Tally said as I looked over at him in shock. How was he here if he died the same night as Gabby? This day just kept getting crazier.

CHAPTER 5

SIMONE

N ATHAN CONTINUOUSLY HELD me as they all stared at my dad, confused. Wow. My dad. Who'd have thought I would meet my parents after twenty-one years? After the strangest circumstances. This world was full of surprises.

"How is this? How are you here?" Tally and Eva asked simultaneously, taking in his scruffy appearance. Surprise quickly turned into anger.

"You took Gabby away from us," Eva growled at him. "We trusted you."

"No, that's not what happened," I interrupted. "They took him. Chasity just found him literally today."

The structure filled with silence as everyone calmed.

"A lot needs to be sorted out, so we might as well get comfortable," Tally said, followed by a sigh. I looked over at Nayeli, who had been continuously occupied by her phone. I knew Jessie was on her non-stop.

Nathan still hadn't put me down, nor had his grip loosened. I looked over to my dad. "I'm gonna go talk to him, then we can visit my mom." I pulled back to look at Nathan, whose face was buried in my neck. "Go to the room, Nathan," I said, and he immediately did as he was told before kicking the door closed behind him.

"Can you put me down?" He shook his head. I pulled his head away, holding his face in the palm of my hands. I kissed his lips. "Baby, I'm fine. I promise."

His eyes were so sad as he lowered me to the ground, still holding me close. "You scared me, baby. You just disappeared. I was feeling helpless as..." He paused, looking at my neck before tilting my head to the side. Anger quickly replaced the sadness in his eyes. I could literally feel the heat radiating from his body.

"Nathan, it's already been taken care of," I said as he bore into me. His angry expression remained. "I promise."

He flopped down on the bed, pulling the ultrasound from his pocket and staring down at it. Had he been wreaking havoc on Mobile with this ultrasound lingering in his pocket?

Of course, he had. He hadn't even been able to respond after I told him I was pregnant. I was whisked away before he could even process it fully. He smiled briefly at the photos before pulling me closer and kissing my belly through my t-shirt before revealing my bare belly. He kissed it lightly. "A nigga about to be a daddy. If something happens to my baby, I want blood, Simone. I don't give a fuck who she is!"

I lifted his face so he was looking up to me. "Baby, the both of us are fine. I understand your frustration, but I'm right here in front of you. It's not going to happen ever again. It's been taken care of." He tightened his hold around my waist once again. He was going to need continuous reassurance. I knew my man like the back of my hand. He was going to be annoyingly overprotective for a while. "I need to visit my mom, Nathan. My dad really wants to see her, and I know she's going to be angry and have a lot of questions. I think this is something we need to do alone. When we're done, I'll come out and get you so we can go to sleep. I'm tired as fuck," I let him know, already knowing he would try to come along. My parents needed to get past the shock of everything before anybody else was brought into the mix. She was about to be face to face with a forty something year old man she thought died twenty years ago, and he with the nineteen-year-old girl he'd been in love with.

He hesitated for a while before turning and leaving. I summoned my dad into the room and went for the candles. We hadn't spoken much. It was still very awkward between us. We didn't know each other. By the time I returned with the candles, he already sat Indian style on the floor.

"Where'd you get that?" he asked, looking at the gold bracelet on my wrist.

"Found it in your closet. A vision showed me what it was."

"Glad it found its way to you." He smiled, reaching for my hand.

We stared at each other before I cleared my throat. "Umm, let me talk to her first. She thinks the two of you died together. She is going to need a little prep."

He nodded as we proceeded to chant in unison, lifting from the ground and returning to our previous spots.

We opened our eyes, now inside the living room. I stood quickly, heading into the bedroom. If they visited her while I was missing, I was sure they told her what was going on, so I knew she was just as worried as everyone else had been.

"Mom!" I yelled, walking into her bedroom as she emerged from the secret door.

She gasped. "I was so worried, baby girl. Did she do anything to you?"she inquired, looking me over and stopping at my neck. "She did this to you?"

I nodded. Her eyes bucked as she took a step back before placing a firm hand on my belly, eyes closed, chanting inaudibly. She smiled, opening her eyes.

"Guess he told you too, huh?" I asked.

She chuckled. "Yeah, he set all of us straight. That boy really loves you."

"Yeah, I know," I returned, smiling.

"Oh, you know now?" she mocked with a smug look as we both

laughed, which was quickly interrupted by a random noise coming from the kitchen area. She was on alert. "You bring somebody else with you?"

I nodded. "I need you to be open minded and listen, okay?"

She looked confused but nodded in compliance. I pulled the door open, and he stepped into the room.

They stared at one another in shock. She hadn't aged a day, and he'd aged twenty-one years.

"Baby," he said, starting in her direction.

She stepped backward, looking over at me. "What's going on, Simone? How are you here, Chase? Why do you look like this?" She rambled on. The Chase she remembered was a twenty-two-year-old clean-shaven man. The man who stood before her was in his early forties and sporting a scruffy beard and wild untamed hair. *How the fuck did he age?* I heard.

There it was again. I could hear her thoughts. Her voice shook. "Chase! Start fuckin' talkin'. What's going on? Tell me I haven't been over here miserable while you've been living your life."

He shook his head. "No, baby. How could you think that of me?" he asked seriously as she scoffed, motioning toward his appearance. "Gabrielle, you know I love you. Don't question that again. Now, sit down and listen to me, baby." He knelt in front of her as she obliged. "You know how crazy Cheryl is. She's unpredictable, baby. Neither of us could have seen it coming." Her eyebrows knitted. "That night, she doubled back and transported me to a cabin from my childhood. She brought me back before it was too late. She's spent all these years trying to erase the two of you from my memory. It didn't work." He looked back at me, smiling. "If it hadn't been for Gabby Jr. back there, I wouldn't even be here now."

I laughed a little.

"She had you imprisoned? I'm still not following, Chase. You're here clearly alive, and you're telling me she brought you back from the dead? Something we know doesn't work from experience. That's what you want me to believe?"

He sighed. "No, Gabrielle. That's not what I'm saying. I hadn't completely moved on to whatever is after death. She performed some kind of spell I'd never heard of, but it only works while the person is still in limbo. She had that and the other spell she used to try erasing you from my memory on a table in the room she'd been keeping me in." He clasped her hands in his. "I want you to believe I would never abandon my family for anything. You knew that before all this transpired. Nothing has changed. I'm still the same Chase you fell in love with, baby," he finished with pleading eyes.

She lifted a hesitant hand to his scruffy face, caressing it. He kissed the inside of her hand. "I missed you, Chase," she said through tears. He lifted her into his arms as they kissed. I was gonna be sick.

She pulled away, fingering his beard. "You're nowhere near the same Chase I fell in love with. I like this on you, though. Maybe cut it down a little, but I like it," she informed, looking at him like a lovesick little girl. Her facial features quickly changed. "You have to do something about your mom, Chase. Look what she did to my baby's neck." He dropped his head, and she looked back at me. "We're about to be grandparents now." His head shot up to her and back to me. "As long as Cheryl is around, she is a threat, and this will not happen again, Chase. You take care of it, or I will."

They spent most of the two hour visit staring at one another while I spent it staring at him. I had my dad back, and it was still so unrealistic to me. I wasn't lacking in male figures or anything because Daryl, Nayeli's dad, made me feel just as welcome as Eva from day one. He treated me no different from Nayeli, but I had been putting a bit of distance between us since coming into my power. He wasn't aware of any of the supernatural things going on around him, and I didn't want to slip up.

When the candles finally burned out, my dad went out into the living room to make himself comfortable amongst Tally, Eva, and

Nayeli as Nathan and I retreated to the bedroom. There were so many unanswered questions I had alone, so I could only imagine what questions and thoughts swarmed Tally and Eva's mind, but that would all have to wait until tomorrow. Rest was needed by all.

I lay in bed wide awake as Nathan lay on my chest wrapped tightly around me. Everyone else had fallen asleep in the living room, except Nayeli. She must have snuck off somewhere to talk to Jessie because I could feel that she was irritated.

"Go to sleep, Simone," Nathan demanded. I was trying, though. I just couldn't get what my mom said to my dad out of my head. *Do something about your mom, Chase, or I will.* What could she have meant by, *or I will?* What could she possibly do from beyond?

CHAPTER 6

NAYELI

I YAWNED, sticking my key in the lock before it was snatched open. I sighed. I was too tired to deal with his shit right now. I needed sleep. That couch uncomfortably slept four people.

"Please, can we do this later, Jessie? I'm sleepy," I said, walking past him.

He turned me toward him. "You need to stay in contact with me. This shit doesn't need to happen again, Nayeli!" he clarified with finality, staring down at me.

I stare back, annoyed. "Okay. Can I go to sleep now?"

I wasn't up to arguing with his ass today. He could have this one. He was lowkey right, anyway. I had been ignoring him basically since Simone had been missing. My connection to her trumped his, so he had to stay home in wonderment. I knew that was killing him.

"I'm serious, Li," he started, calling me by the nickname he'd given me. "You need to go ahead and set that shit up with yo' momma 'cause I ain't fuckin' with how you're actin' right now."

I grabbed his hand, pulling him behind me to the bedroom. "I already said okay, baby," I whined. "Can we just go to sleep? I'm tired, and you said you weren't gonna stress me." I pouted. He pursed his lips but continued to follow me back to the bedroom. I could tell he hadn't been to sleep either, due to the restless expression in his eyes and the five calls and texts each hour.

I stripped out of my outer layer of clothing and crawled into the middle of his bed as he climbed in behind me. He pulled me as close as possible into him while caressing my non-existent belly. He kissed the back of my neck. "I love you, Nayeli. Ion need you stressing me out worrying about your ass, either."

I chuckled a little. "I love you too, Jessie," I informed before we drifted off to sleep.

A couple of hours had gone by the time I woke up. It was early in the afternoon, and Jessie still laid out across the bed. I stretched for about fifteen minutes, something that had become a habit since my transformations began. I headed into the bathroom to take a hot, much needed shower before heading into the kitchen to get started on some food. I was starving.

I started my playlist on shuffle and moved around the kitchen swiftly, getting all my prep out of the way. It was a little late for breakfast, so I was whipping up a quick lunch.

Halfway through finishing the meal, I felt Jessie's strong arms wrap tightly around me before feeling his soft plush lips on the nape of my neck, then to the left side as a chill ran through my back. I blushed before nudging him away.

"Stop. I'm trying to cook!" I dragged because had I got too excited this meal would have been a distant memory.

He smirked before rounding the bar and taking a seat. "Glad to see you got your appetite back. How did you sleep?" he asked, unconsciously flexing his strong tattoo covered muscles.

My teeth sunk into my lip as I took in his sexy appearance. "Good. I feel really well-rested, babe," I said, picking up my phone to check the message that had just come in.

Bestfriend: Wyd?
Me: Cooking. Want some?
Bestfriend:Yessss! I'm starving.

I smirked, tossing my phone onto the counter, and looking back up to my man as he continuously admired me. I blushed.

"Babe, we're going to take this to go. Go ahead and get dressed!" I said to him as I turned back to the stove.

He rose from his seat. "You tryna get some early practice in or something? You know I like that bossy shit," he said, and I ignored him.

About thirty minutes later, we were dressed, and the food was all packed up. He wrapped one arm around my waist as we jumped back to the apartment I used to share with Simone and Nathan. As soon as I placed the containers on the counter, I heard her headboard bang against the wall.

"Eww!" I yelled so they could hear me.

I rolled my eyes and went over to grab the plates from the cabinet to start plating our food, being the culinary student I was. By the time I finished all four plates, Nathan emerged from the room first, smiling wide.

"Smells good! What's on the menu?" he asked before slapping hands with Jessie and taking a seat as I looked on, disgusted.

"Glad to see you in a better mood, bro. Yesterday you was a different nigga," Jessie said to Nathan, shaking his head from side to side as Simone made her way out trying to contain her smile.

She came over and pulled me into a close hug. Now that Nathan wasn't hogging her from everybody else, we could have our moment.

"How is my nephew doing in there?" I whispered as she laughed.

"He's okay!" she replied before pulling away and going to a seat beside Nathan. I played into that shit for her because she would definitely be having a girl. I could feel it, and I knew she could, too. We sat and ate as if the events of yesterday hadn't happened.

I looked down to her end of the bar. "How has seeing your dad been?" I asked before stuffing my mouth. I felt like I hadn't eaten in weeks, but it had only been a day and a half.

She smiled. "Okay, I guess. It's kind of awkward right now, but time will tell. He and my mom got a lot to talk about, though. She was pissed seeing him all aged and what not, thinking he had been out here living his best life while she sat in solitary," she finished, now stuffing her mouth.

I shook my head in amazement. Our lives were crazy and getting even crazier by the day. Speaking of, I needed to talk to her about my newly discovered ability.

After finishing lunch, Simone and I cleaned up our messes. I washed, she dried.

"What y'all got up today?" Nathan asked, turning on the game system in the living room as Simone and I shared a look of annoyance.

"Meet the parents, bro." Jessie sighed as I rolled my eyes. Before we left, he made me call my mom to let her know I was coming by today to talk. "I ain't going through another day like yesterday. Nayeli ignoring a nigga and shit," he continued as he cut his eyes over at me, and I rolled mine again. He was such a baby sometimes, but he was my baby.

We stayed to chat for another hour before jumping back to his condo and getting into my car to head over to my parents' house. I was a nervous wreck. Meanwhile, Jessie sat beside me cool as a cucumber.

I glanced over at him scrolling through a directory of property for sale.

"What, baby?" he asked without looking away from his phone.

"Jessie, don't forget my dad doesn't know anything about the supernatural world."

He glanced over to me before looking back into his phone. We rode the rest of the way in silence. It was about an hour drive since we were coming from Mobile. I pulled into my parents' driveway and parked before sighing.

He smirked over at me. "Chill out, baby. I can take the heat." He leaned over the center console, kissing me with those sexy ass lips of his. "Come on."

We climbed from the car, and he wrapped a protective arm around my waist as I unlocked the door with my key. I heard them in the kitchen talking and laughing, so we headed in their direction.

My mom stood at the counter, cutting up vegetables with a glass of wine in front of her as my dad sat opposite of her sipping from his glass. I cleared my throat.

"Hey, Mama. Hey, Daddy."

I was a daddy's girl, and he was a girl dad. He had both Simone and I spoiled rotten. They remained silent as they stared at Jessie, who was standing beside me with his arm still wrapped around me. I swallowed nervously.

"This is my boyfriend, Jessie." I looked at my mom. "I think you might know his mom from your time in Mobile, Felicia."

Her face softened as she looked back at Jessie.

"Nice to meet y'all," Jessie said as he followed me to the table, pulling my chair out.

He took the chair beside me as I continued. "There's more. I'm pregnant!" I finished after a brief pause, looking down, twiddling my fingers as I heard my mom scoff.

"Baby girl," my dad said before sighing. A lone tear escaped my eye. I hated to disappoint my dad. "Don't cry, baby. It's okay," my dad said as Jessie wiped my tears away.

"It's okay? What's okay about it, Darryl?" my mom asked my dad as he gave her a look. "What about school? What about your plans? How long has this even been a thing, Nayeli? You were just with Cameron not even six months ago." I saw Jessie's jaw clench from my peripheral at just the mention of his name. "What's the rush?"

"That's enough, Eva!" my dad said as I was now sobbing like a little girl being scolded by her parents, which was the case except I wasn't a little girl. I was a grown woman two months away from being twenty-two years old.

"If I may speak, this ain't no fling. We gonna be together. We're gonna argue, but we're gonna be together. She's gonna finish school. She's gonna open up her restaurant, and Ima keep running my businesses. Nayeli and my babies are going to be well taken care of."

My mom choked on the wine she'd just sipped. "Babies?"

"Yes, twins," he answered, wiping my tears away.

She sighed rounding the counter. Between you and Simone, I don't know which one of y'all gone drive me crazy first. She looked over at my dad. "Oh yeah, *Mr. It's ok*, Simone's pregnant, too."

My dad sighed, turning to her. "Stop! They're both grown. Older than you were when you were pregnant with Nayeli, actually. They're not bringing home babies by random niggas, and I'm satisfied with that. They are grown, Eva. We can't control them forever."

After talking for a little while longer, my dad left to go watch the game with some friends. Now a real conversation could be had. My mom turned the food she'd been cooking down to a simmer and topped off her wine before sitting on the opposite couch from Jessie and myself. She glared, sipping from her glass.

"Twins, huh?" He nodded. "You sound pretty sure about your intentions. How can you be so sure? So early on? I mean, this relationship only has a lifespan of ninety days."

She was really starting to get under my skin with her snide comments. "I'll tell you the same thing I told Nayeli," he started before looking over at me. "I've been in love with her since I was sixteen years old when my grandma showed me my soul mate." I blushed. "All this is sudden to y'all, not to me. For me, it's nine years overdue," he finished as my mom sat speechless. I smirked. He told her ass.

Some time went by before she spoke again. "I've seen visions not come to fruition as they were seen plenty of times before. I'm not saying I have a problem with your relationship; this is all just too fast. Have you even given time to get to know each other?"

"I know everything I need to know about my woman, and she knows everything she needs to know about me. She got unlimited access to me. You may not believe in the vision I saw, but I saw it, and it's here." I stared lovingly at his handsome side profile as he continued. "I didn't know her name or where we would meet. I didn't even know what she looked like at the time of the vision. The vision started with seeing her beautiful face at Voodoo that day. I didn't even know that club would exist at that time. Us meeting was authentic and perfectly timed with her coming into her abilities. Fate already knew how everything would play out for her and Simone as well as her and me."

I was happy he had taken over the conversation. Something about being scolded by my mom always made me shrivel in size.

I instantly got hot as lust rolled through my body. He always spoke about me as if I was royalty or a rare specimen, and that shit turned me on. I leaned over and pecked his lips passionately as he tore his gaze away from my mom to look at me.

Now that I was all hot and bothered, it was time to go.

"Aight, Ma, we gotta get going. We got a long drive back to Mobile," I let her know as I gathered my things. I was ready to go home and be nasty with my man. She packed us up some plates of the food she'd been cooking, and we were on our way.

The ride back to his condo was cool. He was driving now because I was being lazy. He came to a red light and leaned over the console.

"One set of parents down, one to go," he kissed me and turned back to the road. *Fuck me!*

CHAPTER 7

GABRIELLE

THE COOL BREEZE of the wind provided a calm I couldn't give myself. I was spiraling. I lay on the back patio of the cabin looking up at the sky. The bright sun shone down through the fluffy clouds. The trees from the forest surrounding the cabin blew in the wind.

Although I was surrounded by all these bright colors, I felt like I was sinking deeper into a black pit. I was in the dark about everything going on outside of the plane. I sighed. Eva seemed to be angry with me, which honestly was to be expected. I found a way to keep her out of the loop of my plans, and she didn't get a chance to say goodbye or try to stop me. Everything I did in preparation leading to my death was at the last minute, so I had no way of letting them know I was over here... lonely. Chase was still alive. He'd been alive this whole time, and boy did age look good on him.

I had already been trying to find my way back ever since Simone's first visit. I hadn't been to sleep since Simone had gone missing. Now that Cheryl was on my baby's trail, and she was going to be having a baby of her own, I needed to get back so they could have a better outcome than we did. That bitch wouldn't do to Simone what she did to us.

It had been twenty-one long years of solitude. Seeing him again after all that time brought back all these feelings I thought were gone. I sighed.

23 years ago

"Hurry up!" Natalia yelled as I scoffed and continued to get my baby hairs together. My long curly hair was split across the middle in a half up and half down style. I was sporting a yellow bikini with a pair of jean booty shorts. A simple pair of flip flops from old navy and my favorite body spray to top it off. My mocha skin was glowing, and I was looking good on my fuck Cory shit.

That nigga had become the least of my worries, and I was happy to be rid of that burden. Today, Natalia and I were headed out to this lake party. Eva wouldn't be coming, claiming to have to help her mom with something. She always forgot we shared literally everything, so we knew she was really spending time with this outsider boy who knew nothing about our world. Hey, if she wanted to live that complicated life, then more power to her.

"Oh, my God! Could you be any slower?" Tally asked, bursting into my bedroom as I twirled around in my body length mirror.

"Where are you girls headed?" My mom's voice broke through from the doorway before I could respond.

"To a lake party, Mommy. How we look?" I asked, throwing my arm over Tally's shoulder, posing.

She smirked. "Gorgeous! Now, have fun, and be careful." She doubled back. "And Gabby, you know what time to be home. Don't try me!"

"I know, Momma." I smirked, grabbing my purse and my pager. "Let's go."

On the way there, we stopped by the hood store, which was just a shop set up in someone's garage, to get some drinks and weed, then we were on our way.

Upon arrival, I noticed the lake was packed. Everyone who was anyone was out here and then some. Except Eva of course. There were so many new, fine faces I couldn't wait to meet. We walked up to get a table at the picnic area. Getting into that filthy ass water was never a part of the plan. We'd leave that shit to the white attendees.

We rolled a blunt each before leaving the car as well as fixed us a drink. We lived the dream lives of a typical seventeen and eighteen-year-old girl. Being witches allowed us a different type of freedom than a typical teenager would. At such young ages, so much was expected of us, and we all coped with those things in our own ways.

*"Ready or not, here I come, you can't hide
Gonna find you and take it slowly
Ready or not, here I come, you can't hide
Gonna find you and make you want me"*

"That's my shit," I said, rapping along to the Fugees as I pulled on the blunt before passing it over to Tally. I was vibing, which was much needed. I hadn't really been out much because of everything that had gone down with Cory. His continuous shitty actions, along with the others before him, had completely turned me off from men. I wasn't a lesbian or no shit like that, but I was taking a break from them for damn sure. But today was the first day of summer before my senior year, and I was going to enjoy it. I was no longer in hiding.

*"I play my enemies like a game of chess, where I rest
No stress, if you don't smoke sess, lest
I must confess, my destiny's manifest"*

I rapped along to Lauryn Hill's verse. She had quickly become a favorite of mine. The whole scene was a vibe, and I was loving it and disappointed I had been missing out on so much.

The party continued to flow on peacefully as Tally and I partied amongst ourselves as well as others, but mostly ourselves.

"Ur uhm!"

We turned in the direction of someone clearing their throat. I was semi cross faded, but from what I could make out, there was a fine ass white boy towering over our table. The finest white boy I'd ever seen. He had long dirty blonde hair pulled up into a messy man bun. He was shirtless, giving me the perfect view of his perfect six pack accompanied by a few scattered tattoos. He had the prettiest light-colored eyes, and his sexy face was lightly bearded. He clearly didn't attend any of the high schools in the area. Maybe one of the colleges, but I had no idea there would be college kids here.

"Although I have been trying, I haven't been able to keep my eyes off you since the impromptu Fugees concert you put on earlier." He smirked. "My name is Chase."

"Gabrielle," I purred before Tally excused herself. He sat opposite me at the table. He shook his head.

"Sorry for staring, but you're pretty as hell, Gabrielle," he said as I blushed. I could tell this wasn't your ordinary white boy. This one had a little soul in him, *I thought. He had a nice full set of lips and courtesy of the windy weather my nostrils were attacked by his masculine cologne. He smelled good.* "So, Gabrielle," *he started, pulling me away from my thoughts.* "You from around here? I've never seen you before." *I nodded.* "How old are you?"

"Seventeen. You?" I returned.

"Nineteen." He smirked. "Perfect. What are you doing later tonight?"

Who the fuck was this bold ass, cute ass white boy? He wasn't my type at all. Nothing close to it, but for some reason, I was feeling him. "How do you even know I'm single?"

"No man is letting your pretty ass roam around by yourself looking like this. I already want to put you away for myself, but I'm a patient man. So, about tonight?" he asked again, biting down into his full bottom lip. I guess I could take a page from Eva's book and give this regular boy shit a try.

I smiled at the memory with my eyes closed as I enjoyed the stillness along with the breeze, when suddenly, I heard the creaking of a floorboard. I wasn't alarmed or anything, I was already dead. What the fuck else could happen?

I stood from my position to see who the visitor was. Stopping in my tracks, I locked eyes with Chase Blanche, the love of my life, looking as sexy as ever. He cleaned himself up a bit since the last time he visited.

His facial hair was now shaved down a bit. His once scruffy and wild hair was now tamed and pulled back. He had aged so well, but I still could not get over the fact that he had aged at all.

"Hey, baby," he said, taking steps toward me. He pulled me into him as I looked up into his light eyes, the one's identical to Simone's. He leaned down to kiss my lips. "I missed you. I missed so much when she had me locked away." He paused, leaning his forehead against mine. "I missed so much with Simone."

I knew that alone bothered him the most. He was very excited about becoming a dad. From the moment I told him I was pregnant, he talked about being a father non-stop.

"Don't beat yourself up about it, Chase. She understands none of this was our fault. She knows how much both of us loved her. Still love her. Have you two had a chance to talk yet?" He shook his head. "She did have a rocky start with living in foster care." He looked up to me, furious. "But she's been with Eva since she was nine. She and Nayeli found each other. Even though she didn't have access to her magic, they were still drawn to each other. Apparently, Chasity had eyes on her for the first nine years but lost her when she moved in with Eva."

I stared out into space as he lay peacefully against my chest. I wondered what was going through his mind. I loved Chase, but I had time to let him go, and I wasn't too sure how he would deal with not having me around. I hoped he didn't plan to come over here often. The fact that we couldn't control how long the visits would be was damaging enough.

Although it wasn't what I wanted, I needed him to move on with his life. He was alive. I wasn't, and he couldn't live over here with me. He pulled away to look up at me. "The pace of your heart just changed. What's wrong?"

I stared back at him blankly before responding. "Chase," I started caressing his face. "You're going to have to move on."

He sat up completely, still looking at me and frowning. "From what?"

I sighed. "From us. From me." He jerked his head back. "Chase,

I'm dead, you're not. You need to live your life and get to know your daughter, and you can't do that over here with me."

He scoffed, standing to walk away from me before turning back to me. "What changed with us?"

"Umm... I died, Chase. Has that not been painfully obvious?" I asked, eyebrows knitted.

"Nah, don't blame it on that," he stated as I stood. "You tried to leave me before this shit even happened. Left my fuckin ring with a note and took my baby. Wouldn't even tell me to my face that you were leaving. If you don't want me, just say that," he growled in my face.

"You know that didn't have shit to do with us and everything to do with *your* mother, Chase. I put my life in danger to be with you. I'm dead now because of being with you, so fuck what you talkin' about." I pushed away from him and went into the bedroom, slamming the door.

I climbed into my bed, annoyed. Men were so fucking annoying. They took from conversations what they wanted, to hell with everything else said. After minutes, my anger coupled with sadness caused me to doze off.

A sudden dip in the bed caused my eyes to pop open as Chase wrapped his arms around me tightly. "I'm sorry, baby, but you can't say that to me and expect me to react differently. I'll never be able to move on from you. You know how I feel about you, and I'm going to bring you back from over here."

He kissed the nape of my neck. I sighed, settling into his embrace. *Well, it was worth a try*, I thought, but I didn't take his words literally. We'd already been there and tried that years ago with my mom. He was clearly speaking out of emotion.

CHAPTER 8

NATHAN

"Made nigga, so watch how you approach me, I ain't gone play witcha
Look at me and can tell I was made before the wealth
Got so much money I can't spend this shit myself mayne
Lookin' like a rich nigga, glidin' on you bitch niggas, one thing about me I
ain't neva been a bitch nigga
Money in the wall just in case I fall
I know I can't take this shit with me, but still I want it all."

I RAPPED along to Webbie's "Made Nigga" as I backed into my designated parking spot in front of Voodoo. A nigga was in a good mood today. My girl was good, my baby was good. I was good, and money was getting better and better.

I climbed from my money green Camaro and headed inside. I was meeting up with Jessie to go look at some new properties for the gym we were trying to open. We had everything already worked out damn near, we just needed a location. Equipment had already been pre-ordered. Staff had already been hired, etc. I was also looking to get some more property in Prichard Mall, near my mom's hair salon.

That whole strip back in the day was lively and filled with black owned business owners, mostly those of our coven, I was told. Most of the business owners died off during the last witch's war. The mall was filled with different spiritual shops, a soul food restaurant, and my dad's first barber shop location was even over there. I specifically wanted that spot so I could reopen his business.

It was about one thirty in the afternoon, and I'd left Simone's lazy ass in bed napping. I grabbed a bottle of water from behind the bar and headed up to my office.

"What's good, bro?" I asked, finding Jessie stretched out across the couch in my office. I smirked, thinking back on all the times I fucked Simone on that very couch.

"Shit. What's good with you? Finally out of Simone's ass?" he asked, followed by a laugh as he scrolled through his phone.

I pursed my lips, waving that nigga off. He had jokes now, but he had his work cut out for him with Nayeli, so we'd see who had the last laugh.

"Shut up, nigga. How many we got today?" I asked, referring to the properties.

"Just a few. I gotta meet up with my momma and Jordan a little later," he informed me as I flipped through some papers on my desk. I was happy for my boy and myself. We were doing great with our entrepreneurial ventures, together and separately. Both our relationships were growing in positive directions, and neither one of us had to kill a nigga. Yet. Shit was looking up for us all. After finishing up, I locked the files away in my desk and joined him as we descended the stairs to lock up before leaving.

I hopped into his passenger seat, and we were on our way to the first destination.

"How did that shit go with Eva and Darryl?" I asked, smirking a bit. They were on me hard the first time I met them, and Eva had already known who I was. I could only imagine how their meet and greet had gone with revealing she was pregnant as well and with twins.

He sighed, making a right turn. "Man, it ended straight, but it damn sholl ain't start that way. Her momma ain't really fuckin with me, but her daddy cool."

I chuckled, already knowing as we came to a stop in front of this large structure. I got out and looked around, this one had a nice sized parking lot, so I was fuckin with that.

We took a small tour around the inside, and I was already mentally placing equipment around the room. This was only the first location, and that was just today. We had more to look at later this week, so I was going to hold out on making any concrete plans, but if we chose this location, we wouldn't have to do much renovating, either. The flooring looked fairly new, and that would be one less costly thing we'd have to come out of pocket for. They already had the correct light fixtures installed. We'd just have to hire an electrician to come check everything out, but that was already a given.

The next couple of locations we had listed to check out weren't much of a tour and weren't really what we were looking for mainly in size, so we were kind of in and out of those.

We were headed back to Voodoo so I could get my car and Jessie could go do what he had to do today. So far, the first location was my top pick. The others didn't have nearly as much space. I quickly pulled my phone out to check my messages.

Baby: Bring me some wings on your way back home.

I smirked before replying and placing the phone back into my pocket. "What y'all got planned to do before the twins get here?"

"Find us a new spot for one. I'ma let her do that shit, though. Give her crazy ass something to do. Open Nayeli's restaurant and do some damn research," he stated as I looked over to him skeptically before he continued. "We need to find out what's about to happen when we mix species like this." He shook his head. I'd forgotten all about that. How was that shit going to work? "What about y'all?" he asked.

"Definitely find a spot, too. Get rid of her fuckin' grandma.

That bitch gotta go, bro," I vowed seriously as he nodded in agreement. "I'ma try to talk to her about moving back to Mobile. Ain't shit in Evergreen."

That might not take too much convincing now that Nayeli was gonna be living there, too. That way she was closer to her dad and the cabin.

"Aight, bro, hit me up. I gotta go take Nayeli's greedy ass something to eat." He shook his head before we slapped hands, and I climbed out of his car and hopped into mine to head to my mom's crib. I needed to visit with my dad before I went back home.

I parked behind my mom's car soon after, and as soon as I pulled the door open, the smell of beef tips, rice, cabbage, and cornbread lured me into the kitchen. My stomach instantly growled as I made my way into the kitchen where I knew my mom was.

"Got it smelling good up in here, girl," I said as I walked up to her washing dishes.

"You're always right on time to eat, ain't ya? Where is the pregnant, hungry one at?" she asked, looking behind me. I knew she'd have a mouthful for me about that but maybe not.

I smirked. "At home waiting on me to bring her some wings, but this looks better!"

I licked my lips as my mouth watered. My momma could throw down in the kitchen. I was gonna stop back by the club to get her wings before going home, but I knew she'd prefer this, and I was happy not to have to make the extra trip.

She chuckled. "What brought you by today, son?" she asked, looking back at me before pulling Tupperware down to fix myself and Simone's food.

"Visit with my dad," I said, looking off to the dining room before doing a three sixty. Nothing had changed about this place since we moved in here when I was six years old.

She sighed. "Alright, I'll leave you to it. I'll leave the food on the stove for y'all."

I nodded and headed back to my childhood bedroom before

powering my phone down so I wouldn't be disturbed. I closed the door behind me and kicked out of my slides, sitting Indian style on the floor of my dark room. I pulled two fresh candles from the nightstand and lit them. I pulled my dad's engraved pocketknife from my pocket. I rubbed my thumb across the engraved symbol before closing my eyes and reciting the incantation repeatedly until I lifted from and returned to the carpeted floor.

I opened my eyes to find myself in my grandparents' living room. I looked around the living room at all my dad's sports trophies placed perfectly around the room.

"Come on, man, with the cheating," I heard from upstairs. I smirked, headed in that direction.

I found my dad in his bedroom tuned in to NBA Live 2005, the one with Carmelo Anthony on the cover. This used to be our favorite pastime. The floor creaked, and he looked over at me, smiling, before handing me the extra controller.

"Hey, son. You come for your weekly ass whipping?" he asked, chuckling.

I pursed my lips before taking a seat beside him. "Yeah, aight, old man, but nah, I got some other shit to talk to you about, too," I said as we looked at each other before turning back to the game to choose a team. I was the spitting image of this nigga, beside my complexion, which came from my mom. My dad was damn near the color of midnight. He had eight gold teeth, four across the top and four across the bottom.

We sat in silence playing the video game.

"My girl is pregnant," I said right after sinking a three pointer. He smiled once again, looking over at me as I returned an identical one. He'd known all about Simone. Had it not been for me talking about her all the time, he'd still know due to him also being a part of the coven. He, my mom, and Gabrielle ran in the same circle, so he was just as happy about our union as my mom.

My smile dropped as I continued. "So much shit has happened since my last visit, OG." He frowned, pausing the game and turning toward me. "Her grandma kidnapped her, but she's good, and the baby good. Get this, her daddy has been alive this whole time." His eyes bucked. "Right? He wants his momma's head, too, but his sister got her locked away somewhere." I looked back up at him. "I want that bitch's blood, OG, bad!"

He turned the game back on. "Nah, if Chase is alive like you say, let him handle that." He shook his head before speaking again. "What Gabby say? I know she's pissed."

I shook my head as well. "I wasn't there, but Simone mediated that shit, so I don't think it was too bad."

I hung with him a little longer playing the game and talking shit before his timer went off, letting us know we had five minutes before the candles burned out. We stood and embraced each other. I missed my dad and coming over here sometimes just made it worse.

He pulled away, looking at me. "Don't forget what I told you. Let Chase deal with that shit with his momma and tell yo' momma to bring her fine ass over here to see me. She can't still be mad," he said as I frowned. Old nasty motherfuckas.

I dapped him up before he began to flicker, and I was back in my old bedroom. I stretched before standing to throw the candles out.

"Who were you visiting?" Simone asked, startling the fuck out of me. I jumped briefly before turning the light switch on frowning, locking eyes with Simone's crazy ass sitting in the middle of the bed. "Don't turn your damn phone off no more, I've been calling you, and I'm starving. You were supposed to be bringing me some food. Now, answer the question," she finished, cocking her head to the side.

This girl was crazy as fuck. "My daddy," I answered lying back beside her in the old full-sized bed. I did not miss this little shit at all. She crossed her legs and turned toward me. "I go visit with him every week, keep him caught up with shit out here." I closed my eyes.

She quickly straddled me and leaned down into my face. "Why you never told me about this? You never even talk to me about your dad. All you said was he was dead."

I leaned up a little to kiss her lips lightly. She was right. It was a sore subject, and I didn't like talking about it. I missed that nigga, though; he was my best friend. He hadn't been of this world for fourteen years. His death never sat right with me, honestly, and it never would. She leaned closer to my face.

"Another time?" she asked, and I nodded. "Aight, well get your ass up, Nathan, I'm hungry, and I know you haven't even gotten my wings yet."

I smirked, standing and carrying her into the kitchen. "My momma cooked," I let her know, sitting her down on the counter before handing her the Tupperware and a fork.

She flipped the top back, and I could literally see her mouth watering before she dug in as I laughed before starting on mine as well.

"I thought I heard talking. When did you get here?" she asked Simone.

I looked over to her. "Good question. How long was your crazy ass sitting on my bed before I came back."

She rolled her eyes as she finished chewing the jaws full of food her greedy ass had stuffed into her mouth. She wasn't that damn hungry.

"I haven't been here long. I got here right before you came back."

I shook my head as we continued to eat and talk. Before leaving, she fixed us some more to go. I guess I was going to have to take Simone over to visit my dad at some point.

CHAPTER 9

SIMONE

I RELEASED a slow moan as Nathan slid in and out of me. My man was so damn fine. I admired his sexy face. His wild eyebrows, supple lips, perfect bone structure, accompanied by very light facial hair. I reached up to pull his face down to kiss him deeply.

"I love you," I said against his lips before gasping and digging my nails into his tattooed arms.

He smirked. "I love you too, baby," he said, rolling his hips into me. He went down to take one of my nipples into his mouth as I spilled out over his length. He quickly flipped me over to all fours, massaging my cheeks before sliding into me.

I hissed, taking in all of him, as he pummeled my middle. He kissed up my back until he made it to my neck and nibbled on my ear.

"Fuck, baby," he whispered in my ear as he continued while I lay flat on my stomach now, mouth hung. The pleasure following each stroke left me speechless.

"I'm about to cum," I whimpered as he moaned into my ear. I pushed my face further into the pillow to muffle my scream as I felt my orgasm inching up.

We released simultaneously before he lifted me back onto my knees and kissed my clit gently. I jerked forward due to it being sensitive. He kissed his way back up to my ear.

"Don't do that shit no more. You know I like to hear your moaning and screaming," he said, smacking my ass before climbing from the bed.

I, on the other hand, was now exhausted as fuck. Sleep would have to come later, though. I was meeting my dad for a lunch date to get to know a little about each other. I smiled briefly. I still couldn't believe I had my dad in my life. If only my mom could be here, too.

I sighed, standing from the bed, hissing from the soreness as I headed into our walk-in closet in search of today's attire. I decided on a cute, gray, two-piece legging set with a green stripe down the side.

I headed into the bathroom to join Nathan in the shower, where we enjoyed another quickie. No wonder I was pregnant. We literally had sex back-to-back like this every day, and neither of us could ever get enough. After getting out, I spread my favorite body butter across my smooth golden skin before dressing. I pulled my wet hair up into a top bun and did my baby hair.

By the time I'd finished and exited the bathroom, Nathan was dressed in some basketball shorts and tuned into that damn game. I was glad I was on my way out the damn door. I slid into my silver Victoria Secret slides and walked over to him.

"I'll be back in a bit," I said before leaning down to kiss his soft lips. "I love you."

I turned to walk away, and he pulled me back into him, kissing my stomach as I rolled my eyes.

"I love y'all too, baby," he said, smiling up at me. I hurriedly left before I found myself engaged in round three.

After the hour and fifteen minute drive to Mobile because traffic was horrible, I pulled up to the Cajun restaurant I was meeting my dad at, and my mouth instantly watered. I walked in, looking around the room before my eyes landed on him seated alone, fumbling with the new iPhone Chasity had gotten him.

I smirked, making my way over to him. It was hilarious because he was still stuck in 1998, and he and technology had a real beef.

He smiled, tossing it aside as he stood to pull me into a hug. How could I long for something I'd never knew I needed. Hugging him felt the same as when I first met my mom.

I took a seat across from him as the waitress quickly popped up beside our table to take our drink orders. I didn't need the menu. I'd already known what I wanted when we'd first planned it.

"Can I get a mango lemonade and a shrimp po boy? No onions or tomatoes, extra Cajun sauce," I finished, looking up at my dad as she wrote my order down on her notepad.

He smiled over at me. "I'll have the same," he said, handing her the menus before she walked away. "That's your mom's favorite, you know? She makes a good one."

I nodded. "Mine too, and I know, right? She made one for me one time I visited her," I finished right before the waitress returned with our drink order.

"You are so beautiful, baby girl." His smile dropped. "I hate how everything turned out. I hate you had to go through that in foster care," he said as his jaw tightened. *Cheryl's gonna suffer for that shit,* I heard. I still hadn't gotten used to being able to hear people's thoughts. It felt so intrusive, but it wasn't something I knew how to control yet. "I missed everything. There was so much I wanted to show you and teach you."

I grabbed his hands from across the table. "You didn't miss everything. There's still a lot to come." I smirked. "And you can still teach me everything. I've only had my magic for a little under a year, so there's still a lot I need to learn."

His smile returned. "I hear I'm going to be a grandad soon." I shied away a bit, nodding as I looked off to the side. I was a bit nervous now. I didn't know why, though. I was grown, but I still felt like a child who may have disappointed her father. "I'll have a lot to teach her, too."

I looked at him crazily. "Her? No, I'm having a boy, Dad."

That felt good. Addressing him as dad.

I could tell it felt just as good to him as it did for me with the huge smile plastered across his face.

"You'll see sooner or later. Have you had any visions?" he asked excitedly. I nodded. "Future visions?"

I recoiled frowning. "No. Just past. Wow, that's going to happen?"

He nodded as his smile widened. "You have no idea what you're capable of," he declared before we delved deeper into our conversation, which I really enjoyed. We talked about everything. My grade school years, sports I played in school, and all the boys before Nathan, which was weird. He wanted to know if any man had ever mistreated me because he wasn't around to show me how a man was supposed to treat me, but I assured him that Daryl did a good job as his stand-in. We even talked about the fact that mom had told him he needed to move on from her. His whole demeanor had gone sad when talking about that, but he was determined to bring her back. He really did love her.

Finally, the waitress returned with our food and some refills on our drinks. I was starving and had burned off all my energy going round for round with Nathan before leaving the house.

I told him about all my visions and that I had begun to hear thoughts. He told me it hadn't developed fully yet because when it did, I'd be hearing multiple people's thoughts non-stop. I could already feel the headache and irritation that would come with that. Fortunately, he said he'd help me learn to control it through meditation and other calming practices.

When we were done eating, he paid and walked me to my car before pulling me into a tight hug and leaving a kiss on my forehead. "I love you more than you know, baby girl. Be careful!" he said before opening my car door.

I smiled. "I love you too, Dad," I said sincerely as I pulled out and headed to the gas station by Natalia's salon in Prichard Mall to get a strawberry, orange, and green apple Thirst Buster slush. That particular gas station was the only one I knew of that had the strawberry orange flavor slush mix, and I'd been craving it recently. Now, I knew why. I thought of my baking bun.

I quickly parked and hopped out to get my drink. I was full and ready to go back home and lay under my man. As soon as I finished fixing my drink, I reached over for a lid and saw a snack cake floating then disappear. I closed my eyes, shaking my head. I was trippin'. I needed a nap ASAP if I was seeing shit. I quickly paid for my drink and candy bar before making my exit.

Cranking up to leave, I turned to pull out and got a quick glimpse of two kids who looked to be early teenagers appearing at the corner of the street, running until they disappeared again.

"What the fuck?" I said aloud. I must've been trippin'. I shook that shit off as well and headed back to Evergreen.

I sang along loudly and horribly to my playlist, and thankfully, the highway wasn't as crowded with traffic as it'd been on the way down. I'd been on the singer Tink hard lately, and her album *Hopeless Romantic* had been on repeat for a week straight in my car. By the time I made it to my favorite song, "Doggystyle," I was parking in my designated parking spot. It wasn't official, though. I'd designated it myself.

I climbed the quick flight of stairs and unlocked the front door, expecting to hear conversation in the living room because Nayeli and Jessie were supposed to be here, but it was empty and quiet, with the only noise coming from the muffled back and forth Nathan was having with the niggas in his headset as he played that annoying ass game behind our closed bedroom door.

I walked into my bedroom, sipping from my drink, walking past Nathan's annoying ass still playing that dumb ass game. He pulled me back into his lap and pulled my cup up to his mouth, quickly killing off half of it. I frowned, pulling it away from him. He was so aggravating. He kissed my neck with his cold lips, and a chill ran through my body.

"How'd lunch go, baby?" he asked, still leaving light kisses around my neck.

"It was really good. We have so much in common, and we talked about so much." I straddled his lap and kissed his lips. "But we have some other things to talk about. Can you get off the game?" I asked. He quickly pulled the headset off and sat it along with the controller aside, giving me his undivided attention. "We haven't discussed any plans now that there's a baby coming, and I know that was probably because so much was going on, but that's not the case anymore, so?" I dragged.

He smirked. "Besides moving into our own spot, I haven't thought about anything else. All I need you to do is keep going to school, take care of my baby, and stay pretty," he voiced, pecking my lips. "But we gonna have to commute now. We're moving back to Mobile. Everything's out in the open, and there's no reason to be away anymore."

I hope I'm right, I heard.

My face scrunched a bit as I cupped his face, looking into his handsome features.

"I have something to tell you," I said, pausing as his eyebrows knitted a bit. I cleared my throat. "A while ago, but not too long, my magic developed some more. My empath ability, specifically. I can hear your thoughts." His eyes bucked. "Not all the time, and I can't control it yet, but my dad said it's only going to get worse. He's going to teach me how to control it, though."

Damn, I'm supposed to be her protector, and she can hear my worries, I heard.

My eyebrows scrunched as I pecked his lips multiple times before pulling away to look at him. "No, baby, don't think like that. Look at me. You are my protector. The only reason that happened is because I didn't listen to you about Salem and because that jealous bitch, Jada."

He frowned. "Jada? What does Jada have to do with anything?"

I'd forgotten to tell everyone about the sneaky, conniving bitch. If you asked me, she'd gotten what she deserved. Only one I felt for in the situation was her daughter. I sighed. "Y'all can call off that search because the bitch is dead. She told dear old granny I was still alive, and she killed her."

He sat staring at me blankly before anger flickered in his eyes. *That stupid bitch better be happy she's already fuckin dead 'cause I had a slower death in mind,* I heard but decided not to address it.

He shook his head. "I don't even know what to say. Why the fuck would she do some shit like that?"

I scoffed. "Nigga, are you serious? Do you not remember my run-ins with that bitch? She was jealous. Trying to get rid of my ass. This is all your dick's fault!" I finished, scowling as he laughed a little.

CHAPTER 10

NAYELI

TODAY, Simone and I were going out to look at some properties for my restaurant as well as some different houses. Nathan and Jessie put us on house hunting duty. We were both in need of a bigger space. With twins coming, and Jessie predicting more sets in the future, we needed as big a spot as we could find.

Since we were going to be living in Mobile now, I needed to find a new spot for my restaurant. I previously settled on the location Jessie had shown me a while back, but I wanted to choose a closer location. Plus, he had a bigger variety out here.

I looked over at the time on the clock on the nightstand. It was eleven in the morning, and Simone would be showing up soon. We slept late because we had a long night, which started with us going out to eat for a little date, ending the night with three rounds of the most passionate sex I'd ever had. A chill ran through my body at just the thought.

I looked down at him smiling peacefully in his sleep while he held on tightly to my waist. I tried sliding from his embrace. He frowned and quickly tightened his grip before looking up at me.

"Baby, I gotta get up. Simone will be here in a little," I said, rubbing my hand over his freshly cut fade.

I wanted to transform and go for a run before doing anything today, but he completely declined my first attempt to get out of bed.

"Five more minutes, baby," he said, lying back on my stomach and kissing it. I rolled my eyes before scrolling through my phone until I felt his lips on my skin again. He wrapped his arms tighter around me before standing and carrying me into the bathroom. I guess he said fuck those five minutes.

"I need to slide up in there before you leave me for the rest of the day," he said before leaning to suckle on my neck.

We were still naked from the previous night's activities, so he stepped inside the shower before turning it on. He stepped underneath the water and stuck his tongue down my throat. His hands roamed my body as I held on tightly around his neck.

He pulled away to look at my face as he entered me. I gasped as our eye contact remained.

"I'm so happy I ran into you at the club that day, baby." He pumped in and out of me, hard. "We gonna be so happy together, baby." I hung around his neck listening with my mouth still agape. "We gonna always be good. The kids gone always be good. I love you so much, Yeli," he groaned as I moaned into his mouth, pulling him into a kiss.

Knock. Knock.

"Can y'all nasty asses hurry it up," Simone yelled, interrupting us.

"She gone have to wait, baby. They had us waiting plenty of times," he said, biting into his lip and continuously pounding into me.

"Fuckk!" I dragged as my abs convulsed before my body went limp. "I love you too, baby!" I finally responded before he unloaded into me.

He stood under the water, still holding me for a little while, before finally putting me down to bathe. He finished before me and left with a towel wrapped around his waist.

"Yall nasty," I heard Simone say as I turned toward the door to find her standing there with her nose turned up. "Hurry up, bitch. We got shit to do today," she said, taking a seat on the toilet lid.

I quickly finished my shower as we continued our conversation. After getting dressed, we were on our way to our first destination. The both of us were working from lists. Mine was of five commercial properties for my restaurant and three houses to look at. Simone had a list of six houses. We were going to narrow our lists down before we brought the men into it.

I quickly settled on the location for my restaurant. It was the second location I visited, and I texted him as soon as I completed the tour. I didn't even need to see the last three. My heart was set on this one.

Me: I found my restaurant, baby. You should have shown me this one before.

It was spacious and modern. I had already visualized the décor and setup.

Headache: I been told you to look at the properties I had in the city. But you ain't gotta run shit by me. Do your thing.

I smiled, closing my phone out and locking up my restaurant. Ah! That felt good, my restaurant. I couldn't wait to have everything up and running.

We headed to the first house on Simone's list, which was a two story, three bedroom, two and a half bathroom. Of course, she found something wrong with it, so we quickly headed to the first house on my list. I instantly fell in love.

I didn't know exactly how much my man had sitting in his account, but I knew it was a hefty amount, mainly because the minimum bedroom he had me looking for was five bedrooms. I hoped for damn sure there were four rooms for two sets of twins and not four sets. I didn't even want to think about me having four sets of twins..

"Are y'all going to move immediately?" Simone asked randomly. I nodded as we continued our tour. "I can't believe we're pregnant right now. Both of us at the same time. What about school?" she asked, leaning up against the wall.

She was so damn dramatic. "What about it, Simone? You can still go to school, and you're almost done. You have support, so what other excuses do you have?"

Rolling her eyes, she walked ahead of me. "Whateva, bitch!"

I laughed. "Yeah, that's what I thought."

I knew this bitch like the back of my hand. We were sisters. Blood couldn't have made us any closer.

After looking at all the locations, we went to a local BBQ spot. My mouth watered just thinking about the chicken dinner plate. Jessie brought me a plate a while back, and I'd been hooked ever since. I wouldn't be surprised if it became one of my weekly cravings and a regular food spot for since I'd be local.

We quickly ordered and sat out in the car to eat.

"What's next?" Simone asked before stuffing a piece of chicken into her mouth.

I smiled with excitement. "I'm gonna start getting my menu together and ordering décor." I was super excited. Also, the location I had chosen had outside seating, which wasn't even something I originally considered. "Oh, and I'm gonna need you to do a taste test for some recipe tweaks."

She smiled brightly. "I am at your service," she confirmed giddily with her greedy ass. She couldn't blame it on the pregnancy because she was greedy as fuck far before conception.

We finished up our meals before heading to the salon to meet up with my mom and Natalia. I hadn't seen her since the day I introduced Jessie. I was stuffed, a little tired, and didn't feel like going back and forth, so hopefully this conversation would be more pleasant than the last one.

"Hey Ma. Hey, Tally!" Simone said, walking briskly to the bathroom.

It was late, so the salon was closed, and we were the only one's here.

"Hey, Ma," I said after waving to Tally and sitting in one of the salon chairs.

She walked over and cupped my face, staring down at me. "Hey, baby," she said before kissing my forehead and taking a seat in the salon chair next to me still holding my hands. "I'm sorry for the way I reacted. I just want better for you than I had myself, and I didn't express that in the best way." She gripped my hand tighter and wiped my tears with the other hand. "So, twins? And Jessie? He's very defensive of you," she said as I blushed shyly.

I sighed. "Yup! Twins. Guess I didn't read the fine print on him," I joked. Well, not so fine. Hell, he was from a long line of twins, which I'd known. He was my baby, though, with his clingy ass, but I low key loved that, too.

"I guess you're moving. I know he's taking my baby away from me," she said through a shaky voice.

Between her and Simone, I didn't know who was more dramatic. "Momma, I'm only going to be the same forty-five minutes away you drove here today to see Tally."

She just wanted to be able to keep popping up whenever like she had been before.

She rolled her eyes. "Anyway, have you still been transforming? How's your control going?" she asked quickly, reminding me of my development from the other night. "You need to transform as much as you can before you start to show because it's going to be harder to do then," she added, interrupting my thoughts.

"Yeah, I have, but we need to talk about the other night when we were looking for Simone. You didn't tell me I would be able to do anything like that," I said inquisitively. She returned a puzzled look before realization covered her face. "What was that?"

She shrugged. "I don't have an explanation for that one, baby.

I've never done anything like that before." She paused briefly before continuing. "Maybe it was the twins. Unpredictable things can happen when supernatural species mix. You may be taking on their power, or they may be enhancing yours."

I sat looking as crazy as I felt right now before smiling a bit. I wondered what else I could do!

CHAPTER 11

GABRIELLE

I STOOD BACK WATCHING the scene unfold before me. The wailing coming from across the street stilled me and snatched at my heart-strings.

"No. no, Gabby, get up, please," she cried, pulling my limp head into her lap. She rubbed her hand across my cheek. "I can't do this without you."

I wiped the tears from my face and took a deep breath before stepping out. After continuously searching, I'd found a spell that worked to invade Eva's dreams. She was still mad at me after all these years, which she had every right to. I took short steps toward her as my foot swiped a can on the ground. Her head quickly shot up in my direction.

"Who's there?" she asked, trying to look through the darkness. I walked into the light as her eyes bucked. She looked down between me standing under the streetlight and me cradled in her arms. I moved closer and kneeled beside her, also taking in my tragic appearance. I looked over at her. "I'm so sorry, Eva."

Her eyebrows knitted. "For what? What's going on? How are

you here and there?" she asked right before I felt a pull. *Damnit,* I thought. The spell had already begun to wear off.

"I can't explain right now. Come visit me when you wake up. Please, Eva!" I said before I was pulled back into my body. I opened my eyes to find myself back inside the secret layer in the cabin. I sighed before standing and cleaning up the mess I made while getting the spell together and hanging the dreamcatcher back in its place on the wall.

I placed my mom's spell book back on the shelf between my grandmother's and mine. I smiled looking over at Simone's. Her spell book had appeared on the shelf about a month or two ago, and I really enjoyed looking at the spells she discovered or tweaked for different outcomes.

I pulled it from the shelf to look at the notes she added. She would update the notes with research information before attempting the spell. I smiled at the thought. My baby was smart as hell to be a new witch, and she had so much more to accomplish.

My smile quickly dropped as I continuously reread the word underlined at the top of the last entry page. Necromancy? I sighed, looking through the notes she already gathered. I closed the book and headed up to the bedroom to get some sleep, but I'd definitely be having a talk with her about this. Playing with necromancy was very dangerous, and I didn't want her tied to it.

My eyes fluttered open as I lay back in my bed staring up at the ceiling. I sat up swiftly, feeling eyes on me. I sighed as they landed on an angry Eva and confused Simone.

I climbed from the bed and stretched before reaching for my robe. It was a bit chilly in here. I didn't know what was colder, the room or Eva's gaze.

"Hey," I said, breaking the awkward silence filling my bedroom.

Eva rolled her eyes. "Why are you invading my dreams, Gabrielle?" she asked, pissed still. I knew because we'd been attached at the hip our whole lives and never had she called me Gabrielle. Only Gabby.

Simone's eyes bucked in excitement before looking at me. "How? Mom, you gotta show me!" she said before quickly reading the room and excusing herself. "Maybe Later."

I looked back over at Eva, whose energy read nothing but anger. I sighed. "I needed to get you to come over, E. We clearly need to talk!"

She scoffed. "Oh, now you want to talk. Not when it mattered? It doesn't matter now."

"Eva, you're talking like I hurt you intentionally," I said, frowning. "I was trying to protect you, and I did! I will not apologize for that," I forced out between tears. "Had I not disconnected our bond you would have died right along with me, Eva. I couldn't let that happen," I finished as tears flowed freely down my cheeks.

"I felt you die, Gabby. I felt every drop of life leave your body!" she yelled at me. "And I didn't even know what was going on. You lied to me about where you were going, Gabby. How did you really expect me to feel?"

"I was dealing with a lot, E," I whispered.

"Yeah, and you chose to deal with it alone. You ain't have to. You fuckin chose that!" she fumed as we stood in a silent standoff. She was so angry. So much time had gone by, but she hadn't let that hurt go at all. I was the one dead, not her.

I'd grown angry now. I missed my friends and wanted to be able to see them like I did with Simone, but her anger for me outweighed the love. "Why are you so angry, Eva? You're not the one dead! I am!"

She frowned before running toward me at full speed. She gripped my face between her hands, and my eyes rolled back. I used to hate when she would do this to show me a vision I couldn't see on my own.

21 years ago: Eva

I sat in the middle of the living room floor of my small two-bedroom apartment. My little Nayeli had gone to the country with my fiancé to visit his family. I sat in silence trying to focus as tears rolled down my face. It had been a couple of hours since the last time I'd been able to communicate with Gabby. I could still feel her, but it was faint.

I couldn't get her by phone. No one else I'd gotten into contact with had heard from her. Not even Chase, and I was more than worried. I feared for her life and my goddaughter, Simone.

Suddenly, a strange feeling came over me, and it was hard to breathe. I tried to remain calm as I continued my chant. I knew this couldn't have been anything good, but I couldn't stop now, I had to find them.

"Nooo!" I screamed as my eyes popped open. I chanted faster and harder. "No, no, no!" I repeated as tears continued to flow faster. "No, Gabby! Where are you?" I yelled into the empty apartment.

I ran into my bedroom, removing the map and other items from the loose floorboard on my side of the bed. I ran back into the living room and dropped to my knees before rolling the map out. As tears blurred my vision, I took the knife, pricking my finger, poured some of the purple potion over the blood, and chanted just as she had taught me to do a locator spell.

I stood over the map waiting for the blood to move in the direction of Gabby and Simone. The flow of tears grew heavier as I felt the last drop of life leave Gabby's body.

I dropped down onto my knees as I broke down. The blood still hadn't started to move, and I was losing it. I'd crawled over into the corner with my phone continuously calling her and got no response either way, but I didn't stop. Suddenly, I saw the blood on the map move from my peripheral vision.

I quickly crawled back over to the map, trying to clear my vision as I followed the trail with my eyes.

"Bienville Baptist Church," I said aloud as the blood stopped in that very spot. I dried my eyes and lifted the window before transforming into my feline and jumping out.

After running for about only five minutes, I halted in front of the pile of cement as the taillights of a car quickly turned the corner. I quickly changed back into natural form as the sound of police sirens got closer. I ran full speed, naked as the day I was born, flipping over huge broken chunks of cement from the collapsed building.

I stopped, and my hands went up to pull at my short tendrils. I dropped to my knees near Gabby's left hand sticking from underneath some rocks. The beautiful ring her mother had given to her before her passing replaced the engagement ring that Chase had given her.

I pulled her into my lap, crying as I wiped the dust from her face.

"Gabby," I whispered. "Get up, Gabby!" I yelled at her as I continued to cry. My life would never be the same.

I moved away from her embrace, staring at her tear-stained face.

"I lost it. I wasn't right for months after that day, and I had no one to talk to about it. Darryl didn't know anything about our supernatural lives, and I'd fled because I thought I would be next," she cried.

I pulled her into a tight hug. "I'm so sorry, Eva. If I could go back, I definitely would have done things differently, but I wasn't thinking about anybody's wellbeing but Simone's at the time. Not even my own. I just wanted my baby to live."

I opened my eyes, and they landed on Simone. Looking at my beautiful daughter, I didn't regret anything. My main reasons were to keep my baby safe, and I did. I sighed, still holding on to Eva. Hopefully I would have my friend back soon as well.

CHAPTER 12

NATHAN

I STOOD at the top of my glass VIP section looking down at the party we booked for the night. It was a birthday party for a popular clothing brand owner from the city.

Hella money was being made, and the vibe was cool. I returned to my seat to pick up my shot glass. This would be my eighth one tonight, and I was already seeing double. I already couldn't wait for this night to be over so I could slide into my girl. I'd been checking her location non-stop for two reasons: to make sure her sneaky ass was still at home and to make sure no more crazy shit happened. I covered our apartment building with a blocking spell for all Salem witches, but it never hurt to check.

That shit had still been fuckin with me a little. They had gotten too close to our coven... twice. With Simone revealing what happened with Jada, the search was now off. I felt bad for that nigga Charles because he had to raise their daughter alone, but I still didn't fuck with him anymore.

"Bro, this shit is lit!" Jessie yelled over the music, interrupting my thoughts.

"Hell yeah!" his twin, Jordan, said. Them two niggas was way more fucked up than me. My phone chimed.

Babygirl: That party ain't over yet?

Me: Ima leave in about an hour. I just wanna make sure everything smooth before I leave, baby.

Baygirl: Fine. Bring me some wings!

I laughed, putting my phone away. She wanted to come out tonight, but that nausea was kicking my baby's ass.

"How's that gym search coming along for y'all niggas?" Jordan asked. He wasn't into flipping properties and what not like his brother and I. Jordan was more into street life. A damn gangster warlock.

"We already found a location. The equipment is going to be delivered next week," I informed, sipping from the drinks I made and bobbing to the music.

After about an hour of that, I was ready to head out before Simone popped her crazy ass up. I stretched, walking back toward the glass encasing as Jessie joined me to talk more about our gym venture. I appreciated the fuck out of the fact that our parents put us in a position to succeed and continue to prosper because I wasn't the type of nigga who could work any job under someone else.

My face scrunched up as I zeroed in on a floating wallet. I wiped my eyes out a little and refocused.

"What the fuck?" I said aloud, looking over at Jessie, who returned a confused expression. "Aye, you see that shit out there?" I asked, pointing down at the dance floor.

"What the fuck? Aye, back that way by the bathroom, too," he said, pointing out another one. Some witches or warlocks were in here on some bullshit tonight.

We quickly descended the steps leading to our section and split up to apprehend both intruders. Getting closer to the floating wallet, I reached out into a bear hug position and pulled them out of the back door, where Jessie already stood with his intruder.

Chanting a revealing spell, two young teenagers appeared before us, frightened. I snatched the wallets. There weren't many covens in this area, and they didn't really have a local look to them. "Who are y'all, and what coven do you belong to?"

Their eyes bucked as they looked at one another.

"E tell'um say'e haffuh do'um," one of them said as Jessie and I stared, confused. *What the fuck did this lil nigga just say?* I thought as soon as one grabbed the hand of the other, and they disappeared again. There was no sense in even trying, they were lost to us now.

We headed back in and up to the bar to drop the wallets at the DJ booth for the announcement to be made. I threw back about two shots before grabbing Simone's food and heading up to my office.

I'd gotten a bit drunker than I planned to, so I was about to go up and jump home because I was far from being in driving condition. I took one last shot before leaving the cup on my desk and jumping to my crib.

Landing in the living room, I plopped my keys on the table and stumbled into my bedroom. Simone lay tucked under the covers tuned into whatever she was watching on TV.

I put her food down on the nightstand and kicked out of my shoes before climbing into bed in front of her as she rolled her eyes.

"Daddy's home," I said, kissing her neck and caressing her small belly.

She scoffed. "Move, boy! I wanna eat before my fries get cold," she whined as I continued on my journey. "Bae," she got out before gasping as my lips wrapped snugly around her clit. I flicked my tongue over it quickly as she convulsed. She propped her legs open wider as I dug my face deeper. "Fuck, Nate! Stop, baby!" she moaned, scooting backward.

"You stop!" I gritted, pulling her back into my mouth, moaning at the taste. Cleaning up everything she released with my tongue, I kissed my way back up to her soft lips. I took her lips into mine and entered her slowly. "Damn, baby!" I whispered before burying my face in her neck. She wrapped her arms tightly around my neck as I lifted her legs and dug deeper.

"Nathan," she dragged. "Baby, I'm finna cum already."

I lifted up, pounding into her. Shit, I was, too. I took one of her growing breasts into my mouth before releasing deep inside of her.

After a few minutes of us coming down from our sexual highs, she pulled my face up to hers and kissed me deeply.

"Now, get your ass off of me so I can eat," she demanded, and I rolled off her and headed into the bathroom.

❧

I woke the next morning with my head pounding and my memory of last night a bit fuzzy. I knew I'd worn Simone's ass out last night, but the events from the club were a bit confusing. I stretched before getting up and heading to my bathroom to get my hygiene together.

I headed into the kitchen where I found Simone moving around cooking. Since Nayeli had damn near moved out, she'd been forced to not be so lazy. I took a seat at the bar.

"Good morning, baby," I said as she turned toward me looking down. I frowned. "What's wrong?"

She sighed. "That food came back up. I'm making this for you. I'm not about to even try to eat anything else," she said, turning back and fixing my plate before taking a seat beside me.

I dug into my food quickly. A nigga was starving. "Aye, baby I saw the weirdest shit last night at the club." I paused to put more food in my mouth. This shit was good as fuck. My baby could cook, she was just lazy. "There must be some new witches in town or something. I ran up on some kids stealing wallets at the party last night. They were using some type of invisibility spell."

She stared at me with her eyes bucked. "I saw something like that too when I had lunch with my dad, and there were two kids, too. A boy and a girl. Like fourteen or fifteen years old. I thought I was seeing shit."

I sighed. This was the last thing we needed right now. The covens down here had done a great job at keeping the supernatural world away from the public eye, but with non-discrete newcomers, all of that could quickly be blown up. "Ima check it out."

"But anyway," she started before popping some grapes into her mouth. She spread three sheets of paper out over the bar top. "I narrowed it down to these three."

This shit was getting so real. We really had a kid on the way. A nigga was happy as fuck, too. I scanned over the three pages in front of me before cutting my eye over to her. "Which one did you really narrow it down to?"

She smirked, still eating her fruit. "This one!" She pointed to the one in the middle, laughing. I knew this girl better than she knew herself.

"I guess we are moving!"

CHAPTER 13

JESSIE

I STRETCHED across the bed reaching for Nayeli before realizing she wasn't there. I sat up swiftly looking around before the heavenly aroma invaded my nostrils. I smiled before going into the bathroom to take care of my hygiene.

As soon as I entered the kitchen, she was turning away from the stove with my plate. Great timing.

"Good morning, baby," she said to me, putting it down in front of me. I pulled her into me and kissed her supple lips.

She smiled before walking away to clean the mess before pulling her shirt over her head and walking out. I turned in her direction, confused. "What you doing, baby? You not gone eat with me?"

My woman was beautiful. Smooth peanut butter toned skin completely covered her petite yet curvy body. Wild black and blonde curls framing her beautiful face.

She pulled her pajama shorts down her long smooth legs and stretched. "I'm about to go for a run while I still can." She rolled her eyes at me like it was my fault. Like she wasn't fuckin' me, too. "I'll be back," she said before transforming into her small feline form.

"I won't be here, but I'll be back before dinner tonight," I said as she walked over and hopped out of the living room window.

I shook my head turning back to my food. Tonight, we were meeting at my parents' house for dinner. This would be Nayeli's first time meeting them, but she'd met and seen Jordan countless times. They'd already known about her before we ever met. Now that she was finally in my life, shit had been picking up like it was supposed to.

Jordan would be bringing his fiancée as well. Grandma had shown both of us on our 16th birthday who our soulmates were as well as a small glimpse into our future. I wouldn't tell Nayeli, but we were going to have three sets of twins. The first set was going to be a girl and a boy. The next set were boys, and the last set were girls. We were going to have a house full of magic.

Montana, our first daughter, was going to be Nathan and Simone's daughter's familiar. I didn't understand it when she first showed it to me, but now it made sense. I was not sure if any of the other kids would get that ability as well, but they would definitely have magic. My parents couldn't wait to meet the infamous Nayeli. The one who had her baby boy's head gone since sixteen and had been driving him crazier since meeting.

I was in love, though. She was everything I expected her to be and more. She was ambitious, independent, and feisty. My favorite trio. All wrapped into a small sexy package. I didn't know what force was responsible for matching us together, but I was grateful. I'd run through a lot of bitches throughout the state of Alabama tryna get to her.

After finishing up breakfast, I headed into my room to get dressed as my phone chimed.

Nate: Y'all settle on a crib yet?

Me: Hell yeah. I let her do all that shit.

I walked into the closet seeing all her things sprawled out across the area and smiled. I was a bit obsessive of her. I'd been that way since before meeting her. It sounded creepy, but given the circumstances, there was an exception.

I quickly dressed in gray NIKE sweats and a black t-shirt. Today was just going to be chill. I was headed to sign the papers for my baby to be the owner of the building she picked for her restaurant, and we had dinner later.

I rode through the city comfortably in my black on black convertible Camaro with the top back keeping an eye out for anything suspicious. Ever since running into those kids lifting wallets, my head had been on a swivel.

A new coven in town could be bad news or good. As of right now, it seemed all bad. They weren't discreet and openly practiced magic. That would put a target on every magical being in this area if seen by the wrong person.

Once I arrived downtown, I struggled to find parking near the probate court. After finally finding parking, I had about a five minute walk until I arrived where my lawyer stood outside waiting. I was more than happy to extend some of the properties I had to my girl. We were going to be together forever, so if she needed it for anything, it was hers.

My dad had gotten me and my brother into real estate as soon as we finished high school, and once I knew the ropes, I brought my boy Nathan in. We had a few properties we owned together and some separate from one another. My main goal in life was a constant steady stream of income. I wanted to live my life with my family, not waste it away working tirelessly for another motherfucka.

I quickly signed those papers and had them notarized and submitted before heading over to check on the gym's progress. We ended up choosing the first location we looked at for the gym. Nothing that followed its viewing was worth anything, in my opinion. Some of the equipment had already been delivered, and we were having some paintings commissioned to spruce the walls up a bit, and the mirrors had been put in. As soon as I walked in the building, I pulled my phone from my pocket.

Yeli: Bring me some chocolate

I smiled and rushed through my walk through so I could get back to my baby and lay under her before we headed out for dinner. I stopped at a gas station nearby to get her a Snicker and fill up on gas. My car was only at a half a tank, but I liked to keep my shit full at all times. While I waited for my gas to finish pumping, I responded to some emails from people interested in some properties I had downtown. Now that my baby had settled on her location, everything else was fair game, and my downtown locations meant big money.

After finishing, I hopped back into my car and made the fifteen minute drive in eight. I walked into my condo and heard the water from the shower turn off. Meeting her in the bedroom, I bit down into my bottom lip, sizing her up as scattered droplets of water rested against her silky, peanut butter skin. Her wet curls dangled at her shoulders, simultaneously dripping water into the towel wrapped around her body. She blushed before looking away. "Did you bring my chocolate?"

I watched as she spread lotion across her body.

"I am your chocolate," I replied walking up to her as she burst out laughing. I left light kisses around her neck as I stared at her body in the mirror, lingering over her slightly protruding stomach. She was only almost two months into her pregnancy, but my kids were shining through.

"I'm nervous about meeting your parents, Jessie," she said randomly.

I pulled away from her neck and locked eyes with her in the mirror. "They already love you. Just as much as me. As long as I'm happy, they're happy," I answered before tightening my hold on her as she smiled. "Now, come on and cuddle with me before dinner."

She groaned. "No, babe. I'm tired," she whined, already knowing what I was trying to do. "And give me my candy 'cause I know you got it."

I smirked, leaving kisses on her neck. "I got you a king-sized single Twix," I said before pushing my erection into her. "You want that or this little ass Snicker in my pocket?" I asked as she burst out laughing.

⚜

We slept about three hours before getting up to go to my parents' house. I only had to slide back into my slides, and she slid into a comfortable jogger set. Her leg bounced uncontrollably fast in the passenger seat. I quickly grabbed hold of it.

"Chill, baby. You ain't got shit to worry about. Your greedy ass just gone eat and enjoy some adult conversation," I said before throwing my car into park.

"One of the houses I chose is close by here," she said, climbing from the car.

I wrapped my arms around her. "Good, we'll have a babysitter close by." I rubbed her belly and opened the door, letting us in. "We're here!" I yelled as the smell of good soul food invaded my nostrils. I could feel her heart rate quicken. "Chill, baby!" I whispered into her ear before kissing it.

We rounded the corner, where a dinner feast awaited.

"Your mom is a chef?" she asked, looking around the kitchen and dining room area. I nodded, smirking. I kept that commonality about them a surprise on purpose. "Now I'm nervous again." She sighed.

"I hope y'all brought your appetites," my mom said as she entered the kitchen with my dad, Jordan, and his fiancée close behind. She smiled brightly, closing the gap in between us. "You must be Nayeli?" my mom asked before pulling her into a tight hug. She took a step back. "I'm sorry, baby. I feel like I already know you. He ain't shut up about you since meeting you," she finished with a light chuckle.

"Aight. Chill out!" I said, annoyed as Nayeli looked back at me smiling.

"It's nice to meet you, Mrs. Cross," she said to my mom.

"I hope you're hungry," my mom said before leading the way to the dining area. "Jessie tells me you're in culinary school, so I hope you enjoy it," she finished humbly. My mom was a fire cook, and she already knew her food was top tier.

We took our seats around the table engaging in light conversation as Nayeli piled our plates high with the assorted options. This felt great. My life damn near felt complete. The only thing missing now were my babies. I couldn't wait 'til they got here.

After eating, Jordan, my dad, and I left the women to converse with each other. Nayeli had loosened up and was now more comfortable. We went into my dad's man cave, where he fixed us a drink.

"What?" I asked my dad as he smirked over at me.

"You good now? Got your girl finally."

I smirked as well, waving him off as I drank from my glass. I knew I'd been getting on everyone's nerves by talking about Nayeli once I met her. She had a nigga frustrated, giving me the run around. Had we not already been soulmates, I would've thought we'd never get together. I wasn't trying to hear none of that shit she was talking about her ex. His time was up as soon as I saw her standing by VIP in voodoo.

"Yeah, nigga done whining and shit. She's giving a nigga the run around, bro," Jordan said, mocking me. Oh, these niggas had all the jokes tonight.

CHAPTER 14

SIMONE

3 MONTHS LATER:

WE FINALLY STARTED MOVING into our new home, and I was ecstatic. It was a beautiful two-story, three bedroom, two and a half bathroom with a huge backyard and two car garages. I knew my initial reaction to being pregnant was kind of impartial, but now I was sweating my little girl's arrival.

Yup! I had been in denial long enough. Apparently, my dad, as well as Nayeli, had already known there was a little princess baking instead of a prince.

I stood in the doorway of the back-patio doors staring out at the spacious area, already picturing everything I'd be doing back here with my little girl. Nathan's arms suddenly wrapped around my waist, startling me a bit. He left a series of light kisses on the nape of my neck before palming my belly. "What you doing out here, baby?"

"Just looking," I answered simply. I was happy to be able to give my kids what I didn't always have. Love, family, and stability. Up until I met Nayeli and Eva, I had no idea the three could co-exist. If it was up to me, they'd never feel anything remotely close.

"Aye, fool. This is your house not ours. Get your ass back out here and help us!" Jordan yelled as Nathan slowly retreated. Laughing, I turned away from the backyard and headed to finish unpacking the kitchen. It was only ten in the morning. So much had already been done, and there was still so much left to do. Everything was coming together in my life. The only thing still missing was my mom. I loved being able to visit her, but I'd feel better knowing she was on this side with us.

After getting everything moved in, Jordan, Jessie, and Nayeli were on their way, and we were left to settle into our new home. Although it took some time for me to settle on one, I loved everything about it. The outside structure was red brick and black. Every room was spacious. There was a bathroom in our room, one in the hall, and the half bathroom was downstairs near the living room.

I turned away from the kitchen cabinets to find Nathan leaning up against the wall smiling.

"What, creep?" I asked, blushing a bit.

"Nothing. Just admiring the view, baby. You feel up to visiting my dad today?" he asked, catching me completely off guard.

I nodded, smiling before it faded. "Are you going to tell me what happened to him?" I asked skeptically. I didn't want to push the issue. It was clear that whatever happened still bothered him to this day.

He cleared his throat. "Yeah. You finished here?" I nodded. "Come on." He led the way to our newly furnished living room. It was the same furniture from the apartment, but it looked different in this space.

We sat in a comfortable silence for a minute before he started. "My dad was an entrepreneur too, like me. He owned a couple of barber shops around Mobile; had one a couple of doors down from the salon. He started the process of opening a new one close to Satsuma." My eyes bucked as he paused. I knew things changed over time, but not too much. With already knowing how the Salem coven had always been, there was no telling how this story was going to go. "The Salem witches, and white folks in general, were harassing him, but he wasn't worried about that shit, so he kept moving forward with his business plans." He sighed. "One day, he left the house to go work on getting the shop together for its grand opening, and he didn't come back home. We waited for hours and even tried calling but no answer. My mom dropped me off at Jessie's while she, his dad, and some other men from the coven went to see what was going on." He paused again, dropping his head into his hands as I caressed his back in an attempt to comfort him. He sighed again. "They found him strapped to one of the barber chairs. His body was completely mutilated." I gasped. "We were never able to find out exactly who did it, but I know it was the Salem coven. Wouldn't any regular motherfuckas be able to get to him at all," he finished, still holding his head in his hands.

My poor baby. No wonder he didn't want to talk about it. He'd never gotten any closure about the situation and knowing him he was still trying to find out who was responsible for taking his dad away from him at the young age of eleven. I kissed his temple. "I'm sorry that happened to you, baby."

"Knock. Knock," we heard from the doorway, startling us.

"That's my dad, I'll get rid of him," I said, standing.

"Nah, baby, do what you gotta do. We got all day." He kissed me before heading upstairs. I sighed, looking up at him. My poor baby.

"Hey, Daddy," I greeted, smiling as I rubbed my belly.

"Hey, baby girl and lil' baby girl." He smiled, touching my belly as well. Our relationship had gotten so much better over these past couple of months. We talked every day and saw each other at least once a week. We had a lot of lost time to make up for. A lot to learn about each other.

"What brings you by?" I asked, easing back onto the couch. This visit was unannounced, and we literally just moved in today, and nobody knew where we lived, meaning he had to have done some type of spell to find me. It had to be important, and I was all ears.

He turned toward me. "I'm going to try to bring your mom

back." My eyes bucked. "I hate having to go to the Ancestral Plain to see her. I want her here so we can finally live our lives together."

I smiled. "Okay, but how? I've been looking into it. Through my ancestors' spell books, but I keep coming up with nothing," I finished, defeated. My spell book was filled with research about necromancy.

He smiled. "You've gotten further than me. I'm still a bit rusty. We're going to figure it out, though. So, this is your new home, huh? I'll have to stop by once you guys get settled." He stood. "I know this visit was unannounced, but your mom has just been heavy on my mind. I miss her."

"It's okay, Dad. I'm always happy to see you." I peeked up at the stairs to make sure Nathan was out of earshot. "You knew Nathan's dad, right?" He nodded, and I explained everything to him that Nathan just told me. He was speechless for a moment.

He sighed. "I don't doubt that he's right. My family and coven were into some evil, hateful shit. I'll look into it for him, though." He pulled me into a tight hug, trying not to squish my belly. "I love you so much, baby girl," he finished before leaving a kiss on my forehead.

After seeing him out, I headed up to find Nathan engrossed in that damn game. Nothing in the room had been assembled, but he hooked that stupid ass game up. I sat in his lap looking over his features. Our kid was going to be gorgeous.

"You okay, baby?" I asked, smoothing out his wild eyebrows.

He nodded. "You ready, or you wanna take a nap or some shit first? He's ready to meet your ass, too. The infamous Simone." He smiled at me before I sucked his sexy lips into mine.

"Now is fine," I replied, standing so he could set everything up. I was a bit nervous for two reasons. I was nervous about meeting his dad and because I'd only ever been to one place in the Ancestral Plain. I didn't know what else was out there. To be honest, I didn't really know much about the Ancestral Plain at all.

He held my hands as I eased down onto the floor across from

him, rubbing my belly while he pulled out the pocketknife that he always carried. Grabbing one of my hands, he chanted as we rose from the floor and back.

I opened my eyes reluctantly, taking in the unfamiliar room. He hopped up before helping me up as well.

"For the threeeeee," I heard in the distance as I looked over at a smiling Nathan.

"Come on, baby," he commanded as he guided me up the old rickety stairs in the fairly old house. "This is my grandma's house and where my dad is linked to in the Ancestral Plain. What's up, OG?" he greeted as he entered the bedroom turned man cave.

He double took before standing and smiling, showing off a mouth full of gold shining through his chocolate skin. He and Nathan shared all their facial features. Height. Build. Their only difference was in complexion. Nathan wore Natalia's bronze complexion, while his dad was a smooth midnight complexion. He was just as handsome as Nathan.

"Simone." He started in our direction. "It's good to finally meet you. I feel like I've known you all your life." He chuckled looking over at Nathan, who rolled his eyes. "All he do is talk about you."

"Aight, nigga, that's enough," Nathan said, cutting him off.

"This my first grandchild?" he asked softly, caressing my protruding belly.

"And only," I added as Nathan and his dad shared a look before smiling. They clearly knew something I didn't. "Anyway, it's nice to meet you, too."

I took a seat on the sectional up against the wall as we quickly fell into conversation. His dad was really cool, and I loved their relationship. I could tell he really missed his dad. My baby and I had more in common than we could have ever imagined.

"I always knew you two would end up together." He smirked. "I told Gabby that as soon as she found out you were a girl. Even after everything happened, I knew you two would find your way to each other." He paused briefly before continuing. "And for the record, I told this nigga to tell you the truth about everything when y'all was only six months into the relationship. His mama would've been okay. I could've taken care of the little attitude she would've had as a result." He smiled as Nathan's face contorted in disgust, and I laughed loudly.

"Aight, nigga, that's enough!" Nathan warned.

I checked in and out of the conversation as I continuously surveyed my surroundings. This had only been the second location I'd visited in the ancestral plane, and I was still learning about it. I guessed everyone over here chose where they spent eternity. My mom's choice was the hidden cabin, and his choice was his childhood home.

I gazed at the many trophies and medals for various sports, but mostly track and football, with the name Johnathan Harris gracing all of them.

"Me and Gabby have always been cool because of your mama," his dad said, looking over at Nathan. "You couldn't have one without having to deal with the other two. I'm sure Chase and Daryl can tell you that, but I was skeptical about the white boy, especially with how things were during those times."

The timer going off interrupted the story he'd been telling us about the first time he and Natalia went on a double date with my parents. My head quickly swung left to right in a panic.

"Chill, baby, that's just letting us know we got five minutes left," Nathan let me know before standing and pulling me up as well.

His dad pulled me into a tight hug. "Don't be a stranger now, Simone, and bring my granddaughter over to see me when she comes. Tell your parents I said what's good?"

"Will do!" I said, smiling and stepping aside for them to say their goodbyes. Suddenly, we were back in our new bedroom. We sat staring at one another for minutes before I finally broke the silence. "Your daddy fine as fuck!"

His nose turned in disgust. "Don't let my momma hear you say that. She'll still fuck somebody up about that black ass nigga," he replied before standing and reaching out to pull me up from the floor.

He wrapped his arms around me, leaving light kisses on my neck as I quickly melted in his embrace. I took a step back feeling his manhood grow. "Nah. I'm about to go cook. You need to go ahead and put the bed together, and don't get back on that damn game until you're done!" I ordered, heading back downstairs.

I could get with this mommy shit!

CHAPTER 15

NAYELI

"PUT those up against that wall and the next set up against this one," I instructed the movers delivering my restaurant furniture as I sat near the hostess podium.

Everything was coming along so well. If things continued to move according to plan, we'd be open for business in a month or two. My menu was coming along great. Later today, Jessie, Simone, Nathan, Jordan, and his fiancée, Reign, were coming by later to try out some new dishes I was wanting to add to the menu. All the décor had been delivered as well as outside seating.

The old wooden bar top had been replaced with granite. Four flatscreens hung from the walls. I'd had a speaker system installed throughout the inside and out, and all new kitchen appliances.

When they were done bringing everything in, I signed off on it and locked up before heading into the kitchen to start cooking before my feet started hurting.

I'd gotten so big and looked to be about seven months, but I was only four. I turned on my playlist and quickly prepared the dinner for six: appetizers, entrees, and desert. Looking over at the clock, I noticed I had a couple of hours before everyone arrived and decided to run over to Target. I was also decorating our new house. Yeah, Jessie kept me very busy. Like I figured, we'd decided on the house closest to his parents.

Unfortunately for my dad and Jessie's credit cards, there was a Target five minutes away from my restaurant. Pushing the basket through home décor, I paused, scrolling through my photos to match some colors for my living room.

"I know you fucking lying, bruh," Cameron's voice rang out, startling me as I hesitated before looking up, avoiding eye contact. The guilt was all over my face. He chuckled angrily. "You can't even fuckin' look at me. You gone cheat on me and let the nigga get you pregnant?" he fumed, walking closer to me.

"I didn't cheat on you, Cameron."

He stared at my belly. "How do you know it's not mine?"

Suddenly, one of them kicked as if they could sense their dad's enemy nearby. I hissed. "I'm only four months." He frowned. "It's twins. I'm really sorry, Cameron. I never meant to hurt you. I really did love you."

"Fuck you, Nayeli!" he said calmly before looking away from my belly to my face. "You say you ain't cheat on a nigga, but either way, you broke up with me because you say you ain't have time for our relationship. Yet, here you are in another one. With fucking twins on the way. But you fuckin loved me?" he yelled, causing me to jump slightly as I looked around for any nosy bystanders. "Fuck you, Nayeli!" he yelled again before his lips quickly clamped shut and thread began to sew through them.

My eyes bucked in shock as he stared back, his eyes bucked in fear. I looked down at my belly.

"No, stop it!" I said to the twins before looking back to Cameron struggling before bolting as fast as my waddling body would allow, heading back to the restaurant.

I went into the bathroom looking at my belly in the mirror, caressing it as four little handprints could be seen clearly through my skin.

"I can't believe you two did that," I said aloud to them. My abilities had continued to grow as well as theirs, all thanks to them. They were already protective and defiant, which was definitely going to be a problem later, but Jessie didn't see the problem with that. As if he could sense me thinking about him, my phone chimed.

Headache: Wyd? Your ass ain't checked in all day.

He was so annoying, overprotective, and defiant. No wonder he ain't see the problem. I rolled my eyes before heading back into the kitchen to start on dinner. My phone chimed again.

Simone: Open up!

I quickly let her in. I sent her a text on the way back that I wanted her to come early.

"Where's Nathan?" I asked.

"He's going to come later with Jessie. What's going on with you?" she asked skeptically after looking my appearance over. She joined me in the kitchen so I could finish dinner while recounting my run-in with Cameron.

She sat speechless as I slid the pan of Salmon into the oven to keep warm. "Wait, so the twins did a spell on Cameron? They're not even born yet, Nayeli, and they won't even have access to their magic until they're sixteen," she tried to reason.

"It was them, Simone, and it's not the first time they've reacted to things going on out here. They are enhancing my abilities as well. Ever since the night you were missing. That was the first time I noticed. Whenever Jessie's getting on my nerves, they mess with him, too." Her eyes bucked as she rubbed her belly. "But this is the first time something was done to someone outside of the supernatural world. How am I going to explain that?"

"Maybe you won't have to. Nathan can wipe his memory again."

My eyes bucked before shaking my head.

"Jessie will probably try to kill him if he finds out. No! He's been looking for a reason. Don't even bring it up to them yet," I said as soon as a message came in.

Headache: You gone make me fuck you up ignoring me and shit. Unlock this damn door!

I rolled my eyes away from my phone, locking it. "That's them. Will you let them in? And nothing about Cameron, Simone," I warned as she rolled her eyes before retreating.

I went to pull out the rolled silverware and glasses.

"Nayeli, you're gonna get enough of playing with me," Jessie's voice rang out before I felt his arms wrap around me then a kiss on the nape of my neck. "I haven't heard from or seen you since you left this morning."

I rolled my eyes before turning in his arms. "Hello, Jessie. I was busy. Did you not see the furniture out in the dining area? Do you not see this three-course meal for six?" I questioned before I was lifted onto the countertop as his tongue forced its way into my mouth.

"Shut up!" he said after pulling away and rubbing his hand up my dress on my bare thighs.

"Woah, Woah!" Jordan interrupted. "Not by the food, man." I turned, smiling as he returned a disgusted look. He and Jessie were identical. Had Jordan not had shoulder length locs, I was pretty sure it'd be challenging telling the two apart. "Can y'all wrap that shit up? We are ready to eat out here."

I brought out the tray of appetizers as Jessie carried the drink glasses and a bottle of wine. Simone and I would be drinking water. Even though the doctor had given the okay for a glass of wine a day, Jessie nor Nathan were going for it. That was just an argument that was not worth it.

"That shit was good as fuck, sis. You tryna give moms a run for her money, huh?" Jordan asked before polishing off the rest of his wine.

I smiled wide. "Really? So, the tweaks to the recipe were good?" I asked Simone. She'd been the only one to taste the first draft.

She nodded. "Yeah, this is it!" she informed me before stuffing seconds in her mouth. I was all smiles. I couldn't wait for my grand opening. I was hoping the people would love my food just as much as my family did.

"Are you two going to join us to celebrate Mardi Gras this year?" Reign, Jordan's fiancée asked aloud as Simone and I looked at each other with the same look of confusion. "Wait, do y'all even know what Mardi Gras is?" she added as we both shook our heads simultaneously before looking over at Jessie and Nathan. They had been holding out on us.

"Y'all niggas been holding out on us?" Simone asked, full of attitude. "I don't even wanna talk to y'all about it." She rolled her eyes away from Nathan and over to Reign. "Is it like the New Orleans Mardi Gras?"

Reign and Jordan's mouth fell agape as they looked over at Jessie and Nathan. "Y'all should be ashamed of yourselves. Y'all ain't tell these girls nothing about where they come from." Reign mugged them before continuing. "Mardi Gras originated here in Mobile. Other places have their own celebrations, and for whatever reason, New Orleans is known for it, but ain't no Mardi Gras like ours. It's a month-long celebration, but the only days that matter are the last three," she informed us.

We continued discussing plans for the upcoming Mardi Gras celebration before we began to wrap up dinner. Simone helped me clear the table while everyone else sat around continuing conversation over more glasses of wine. "Now, I just gotta finish the rough draft of the menu design and send it over to—"

"Hold up. You hear that?" she asked, interrupting me.

"Hear what, bitch?" I asked, annoyed. This pregnancy had me extremely short tempered. I watched as she inched over to the window.

She gasped before looking back at me. "It's those kids again. What are they doing back here? Come on, let's see where they're going." She headed over to the backdoor. "Come on, bitch, before we lose them."

I sighed, following her out of the kitchen door. I knew we'd regret this. If not for the danger we were probably walking into, definitely for the tongue lashing that would come from Jessie and Nathan when they discovered we left.

We tiptoed behind the duo, keeping a safe distance as they surveyed their surroundings before walking through the wall. I looked over at Simone suspiciously before she chanted an incantation after grabbing my hand. We quickly became invisible, and she guided us through the wall as well.

My eyes bucked as I froze, looking around at hundreds of people. Young. Old. Even babies and toddlers.

"What the fuck is this?" Simone thought.

"I think we found their layer," I replied telepathically. Our gaze followed the two kids around the structure, handing out food and water to the kids first, then over to the old. *"Come on, let's get out of here,"* she thought before pulling me back through the wall, and we reappeared. "Come on, let's get back to the restaurant before them crazy ass niggas notice we're gone."

"Too fuckin late!" Nathan gritted, staring from a couple feet away as we froze in place. Jessie was fuming beside him. "You ain't gonna be satisfied until I lock your ass up for the rest of this pregnancy," Nathan added, closing the space between us.

Meanwhile, Jessie's eye contact never broke. He had to be pissed to the highest level because he'd yet to say anything. No yelling. No threats. I knew he'd lay it on thick by the time we made it back home.

CHAPTER 16

GABRIELLE

I MOVED around my garden swiftly, pulling up fruits and vegetables before replanting. I loved being out here, it helped me think and focus my thoughts instead of them being all over the place. Before the reemergence of my daughter and fiancé, I was content with being over here alone constantly. But now, I just wanted to be in their presence all the time. And my granddaughter... I was going to miss so much with her, same as with Simone.

Dusting off my hands, I picked up the basket of fresh produce and headed back into the cabin to whip up a quick breakfast. Simone was supposed to be coming by this morning for a baby update, but I wanted to also talk to her about her necromancy research. I wanted to be with them just as much as they wanted me to, but necromancy was a very dangerous practice.

I wasn't trying to miss out on my granddaughter's life. I wanted to be there for everything. Fate couldn't have worked less in my favor. How was it that both Chase and I were to be executed yet I was the only one dead? I remained salty about that. My life had been taken at such a young age. All for falling for a boy from the wrong side of the tracks.

My mom always warned me before she died that no good would come from being with Chase. She didn't necessarily dislike him, but she wasn't his biggest fan, either. She just simply respected my decisions. I sighed. I missed my mom so much. I missed both of my parents. My dad, Gabriel, died when I was only eight years old. Up until then, I'd been a daddy's girl, but my mom and I had one another to help us get through his death. My mom's death left me feeling alone and had changed me. Nightmares had taken over my life as well as the task of trying to bring my mom back. I'd already gone down this road before, which was why I was so worried about Simone. I didn't want it to consume her like it'd done me.

"Mommy!"

I smiled, wiping the peppers I started cutting up from my hands. I loved hearing her call me that. Like she was still a little girl, but she would always be my little girl. Rounding the corner, I gasped.

"Hey, Auntie Gabby." Nayeli waved shyly as I took in her protruding belly. She was huge. I had no idea how the both of them managed to get pregnant at the same time. Eva was a year older than me, and Nayeli was about six months older than Simone. I approached them with my arms outstretched. "Oh, my goodness. Look at you girls." I pulled away to take their bellies in again. "And Nayeli, you're huge. I heard one of Felicia's boys got a hold of you," I mentioned as she blushed.

"Yes. Jessie, and I'm only four months along. It just looks like this because they're twins.

I smiled, taking the duo in. "Well, come on. I was just starting on breakfast." I turned to head back into the kitchen to hurry through breakfast. We'd only have two hours together. "What have you ladies been up to?" I asked as we sat around the table eating and conversing.

"Well," Simone started before trying to swallow all the food she'd just stuffed in her mouth. "Nathan and I just moved into a new house." She beamed before taking a bite of the crispy bacon.

"Me too!" Nayeli added. "Jessie and I just moved into a five-bedroom house. What do you think he has planned for my womb? Because why do we need so many rooms?" she questioned as I laughed heartily in response. These kids were something else. "Oh, and I'm opening a restaurant soon. The menu is just about ready, but I haven't settled on a name yet."

"I don't have any career plans to brag about. I wanted to be a chemistry teacher at some point because I love experiments." She paused as we smiled at one another. "But with how my life turned upside down in the last year, I just rather focus on this. Understanding my life is more important."

I pursed my lips. "And I'll just bet that Nathan loves that plan, huh?" I asked as she blushed in response. I knew eventually Nathan would try to turn her into a housewife but was unsure if she'd welcome the idea . I knew he'd grow to be just like his dad, who also tried to turn Natalia into one, but she already had her heart set on Cosmetology.

"Tell me about Jessie. How did you two meet? I remember seeing the twins when they were around two or three."

Nayeli blushed instantly at the mention of his name. "It was actually crazy how it all happened. I ran into him at the club he has with Nathan, and he had been stalking me ever since. If I hadn't had a boyfriend at the time, I would have given him a chance sooner, though. He was so handsome!" She stared off into space smiling as Simone and I shared a look.

"Wait, you had another boyfriend?" I asked, eating more of my food, trying to get all the juicy details of this tea.

She rolled her eyes. "Yeah, it ended badly, too. I didn't want to end it initially, but then I found out about all of the supernatural stuff, and I didn't want to live my life tiptoeing around him. I know my mom does it with my dad, but she's been supernatural her whole life."

I nodded in agreement. That made a world of difference. "So, a stalker huh?"

We all laughed in unison.

"Yes, and kidnapper. He was convinced we were soulmates because of a look into the future his grandma gave him for his sixteenth birthday. He said he'd been seeing my face in his dreams ever since." She blushed. "So, while I was still with Cameron, he kidnapped me from school and took me out on dates to get to know *his future wife,* and I fell hard for him. And fast! And now we're about to have twins."

"Yeah, the first set!" Simone blurted before laughing hysterically.

I smirked, knowing Eva had to have shit a brick upon learning of Nayeli's pregnancy. She expected everything in life to be traditional, always, but she was in love. You could see it all over her face when speaking of him.

I loved this; having girl talk over breakfast with my daughter and niece. I wanted more of it. The room filled with silence as they tore into their food, and I focused in on Simone, remembering the things in her spell book. I cleared my throat. "I do need to talk to you about something, Simone."

"Huh?" she inquired, looking up from her plate with a jaw full of food, eyebrows raised. She looked just like me whenever I thought I was in trouble.

She looked over at Nayeli like a sibling needing assistance. "You know, everything you do or leave in the cabin over there, happens over here, too." I paused, pulling her spell book from the chair beside me and sitting it in the middle of the table as her eyebrows dropped in confusion.

I flipped it open to the marked page, sighing at the notes she must've added last night because I'd checked it before going to bed. "I need you to stop looking into this, baby girl." I pointed at the words on the pages of the opened book.

Her face saddened as she looked up at me. "Why? You don't want to come back and be with us? With me and dad?"

"No, no! That's not it at all," I started as I rounded the table, kneeling in front of her. "Playing with necromancy is very dangerous, baby girl, which is how I know Nathan has no idea about you looking into it." She shied away a bit.

"But I want you to come back to us," she cried. "I want my baby to know you because I didn't get that opportunity, and I'm not doing it alone. Dad's helping."

I froze before standing. "He's what?" I asked as calmly as I could because I wanted to spazz. I knew I'd failed at talking him out of it, but that was him. I had no idea he'd try to rope my baby into it.

"Mom, are you mad?" she asked as I noticed the table shaking under my palm.

I quickly removed it. "Not at you, Simone, but Chase knows better." She frowned once again as I returned to my seat. "My mom died around the same time I found out I was pregnant with you, and I fell into a really dark place for the first three months. I stayed in this cabin alone for those three months trying to find ways to bring my mom back. After so long, that was all I was concerned with. I stopped talking to your dad, I hadn't taken any vitamins, and I missed a lot of doctor's appointments," I said with my head down in embarrassment. "Even after pulling myself out of that dark place, I continued trying everything I could find to bring her back, and nothing worked. My last attempt was when I was eight months pregnant, and the spell knocked me unconscious for two days." Her eyes bucked. "After that, Eva put a stop to it. She could feel how it was taking a toll on me." She lowered her head in defeat. "I understand how you feel, Simone, but I've already been down that road, and it's a dead end every time. I don't want that for you. At least we have this," I referred to the ancestral plain. "I don't have this with my mom, so this is just going to have to be enough."

She wiped her tears away before speaking. "You never talk about her or your dad. Why? What happened to them?" she asked before putting a spoonful of grits and eggs into her mouth.

"It's just a sore subject for me. I never knew what happened to my dad. My mom only said he died. I never saw a body or went to a funeral. My mom, on the other hand, wasn't sudden or anything. She wasn't killed. I just simply wasn't ready to not have my mom around anymore. For a long time, all we really had were each other, and I was about to be a new mom. I was terrified. It was cancer, though. She'd gotten very sick, but she was happy to hear about you. Telling her I was pregnant was the first time I'd seen her smile since she'd been sick."

I still missed my mom after all this time, and it would forever bother me that I wasn't able to bring her back to me. That she was also never able to meet her granddaughter or great granddaughter. I shook the emotion away. "Can we change the subject? And promise me you're done with this necromancy mess."

I waited for her response with pleading eyes.

She sighed. "Okay, I promise," she said before stuffing her jaws again.

"Oh, there's a new coven in town!" Nayeli blurted, succeeding at changing the subject as she had my undivided attention. A new coven in town most likely meant trouble.

She looked at Simone to further explain. "We don't know much about them because they're hiding out. We've only seen two teenagers out and about. Nathan and Jessie caught those same teenagers lifting wallets at their club. They've just been using magic very recklessly in public. Nayeli and I followed them into an abandoned warehouse and found the rest of them. Hundreds. Young and old."

"Black?" I inquired. She nodded. That eased my worries a little, but still, who were they, and why were they in town? With those numbers, it seems like they migrated from wherever they called home before.

Suddenly, it clicked. She'd said they weren't being discreet, like they'd come from a place where their magic wasn't an issue. I had a hunch but was unsure, so I decided to keep it to myself.

"Keep an eye on them, carefully!" I warned, looking between the reckless, sneaky duo, thinking of that Salem shit she pulled.

CHAPTER 17

NATHAN

I SAT on the couch playing the game as Jessie and Jordan talked shit in my ear through the headset. I cut my eye at Simone moving around the kitchen making brownies, her latest craving.

That crazy ass girl was a master at getting under my skin. All that reckless ass moving around was already bad enough before, but now she was carrying my kid and needed to kill all that extra shit.

"You suck ass my nigga," Jordan yelled through the headset as I focused back into the game watching the instant replay.

I checked out completely, thinking about the shit she always got herself into. I cut my eye at her again.

"Stop fuckin lookin at me like that, Nathan!" she yelled. "It's been three days, and I told you everything. We weren't even in danger," she finished, slamming the drawer after pulling out a spoon.

"I'ma fuck with y'all boys later," I said to Jessie and Jordan, who were clowning me on the other end because she'd just snapped. I placed the controller and headset on the living room table before trekking into the kitchen. "Calm all that shit down," I demanded as she glared at me from the opposite side of the kitchen's island.

"And I don't give a fuck if y'all weren't in danger. You ain't knew that shit before you walked your nosey, hardheaded ass in that motherfucka."

She pissed me off all over again acting like I was overreacting or something. Jessie and I had these two sneaky motherfuckas confined to the house. The only places they were allowed to go was to visit Gabby, Eva, and doctor's visits.

"Roll 'em again," I threatened, closing the gap between us, referring to her rolling her eyes.

"Tally know you tryna keep me in this damn house against my will?"

"I ain't tryna do shit. Your ass ain't leaving this motherfucka," I let her know with finality as she pouted, turning away from me to pour the mixture into the pan.

I wrapped my arms around her, caressing her belly as she tried to nudge me off, but I tightened my grip.

"I'm not going to do anything crazy, baby. I just need to go to the store," she whined as I ignored her pleas, still leaving kisses around her neck and inhaling her scent. She smelled good enough to eat. Realizing I wasn't going to respond, she pushed me away and slid the brownie pan into the oven.

As soon as she turned around, I lifted her onto the island and sucked her lips into my mouth before pulling away. "I don't care what you is or what you ain't gone do. You ain't leaving this house, though," I informed as she frowned with her lip poked out whining again. "Shut up!" I lifted her bridal style and headed up to our bedroom. We had about twenty to twenty-five minutes before those damn brownies burned.

I lay her back on the bed gently, hovering and leaving kisses on my way down her body. I pulled the oversized t-shirt over her head, leaning down to leave a series of kisses around her belly. Then down to pull her panties off, wasting no time sucking her swollen clitoris into my mouth.

"Mmhm," we moaned simultaneously. I ran my tongue slowly

from her hole to her clit before flicking my tongue across it rapidly as she gasped, scooting away. I pulled her back to me.

"Stop running. You know better!" I wrapped my lips around her clit. Her eyebrows scrunched as we made eye contact while I devoured her. Her eyes closed as her head went back, and her back arched off the bed.

"Fuck!" she yelped, holding the bottom of her belly before exhaling, releasing her orgasm onto my face.

I sat up, solid as stone, and wasted no time sliding into her slippery, warm, Nathan sized walls. She gasped again as her mouth hung open, and her eyes popped open as well.

"Nathannn!" she whined.

I wrapped my hand lightly around her neck and sucked her left nipple into my mouth before kissing a trail up to her ear.

"You better be glad you're pregnant 'cause I'd really fuck you up right now," I whispered before pushing as deep as I could into her as she moaned, tapping on my arm to let up.

"You gone start doing what daddy tells you?" I asked, rolling my hips into hers.

"Yes, baby, yesss!" she yelped as I felt her second orgasm spill out around me, and I filled her up with mine. I pulled away and looked down at her breathing heavily with low lids. Good, her ass would be asleep soon, and all that talking crazy shit was over with. I came back with a towel as she was climbing from the bed. "Go get my brownies out of the oven," she ordered before waddling into the bathroom.

When I came back with the plate of brownies, she was sitting up in bed scrolling through her phone. She locked it, tossing it aside.

"Baby, I need you to do me a favor, but you can't tell Jessie about it."

Here we go again, I thought as I sighed, plopping down on the bed.

We flew through the plate while she explained what happened

with Nayeli and Cameron at Target. I was low key amused. The twins ain't fuck with that nigga. I saw where Nayeli was coming from, though. Jessie would definitely kill him.

"Aight. I'll take care of it." I stood, and she was already yawning.

"Don't tell Jessie, Nathan, because I wasn't even supposed to tell you." She pulled the covers up over her shoulders.

"Shut up and go to sleep. I told you I'ma take care of it," I replied as she returned a menacing stare before closing her eyes. I shook my head at her crazy ass and headed downstairs. Those two motherfuckas had barely even had access to their magic for a whole year and stayed in more shit than a little bit.

I prepped for a locator spell to find Cameron. I hadn't really seen him since he moved out. He was a cool dude, so I really didn't wanna see shit happen to him, but he was gonna have to check his attitude with Yeli, or eventually Jessie's ill-tempered ass was gonna to get a hold of him. Had he known the shit Cam said to Nayeli in Target, he'd have done a lot worse than what the twins had done. Nigga would probably be missing his tongue.

I sighed, grabbing my phone, wallet, and keys as his location appeared on the map. After locking up, I circled the property in brick dust. It was usually used to keep people away who meant you harm, but in this case, it was also to make sure Simone's sneaky ass didn't venture off while I was cleaning up their mess.

I vibed to the music as I drove the hour and some change to Evergreen. I wanted to jump, but the nigga was probably already spooked enough. This shit had happened three days ago.

That day had been an adventurous one for the duo. I was still pissed about them sneaking out. Anything could have happened, and they just left without a word to anyone. That was the shit I was talking about. We were only steps away, and they snuck and did it because they already knew how we'd react.

I pulled into the nice apartment complex, which I was guessing was where he'd moved when Nayeli broke up with him. I recited an invisibility spell before jumping to the other side of the front door to check it out before I approached him. The apartment was small compared to our old one, and it was dark. Fast food bags were strewn all over the kitchen and living room area.

The windows had been boarded up from inside. I followed the distant noise into the bedroom to find him standing near the window looking through a small opening in the boards. I bumped the door a bit, causing it to creak as he quickly turned in my direction. Fear clearly shone in his eyes as I surveyed the tiny holes above and below his lip line.

"Who's there?" he yelled, tightening his grip on the metal bat.

I sighed, quickly jumping back outside of the front door before knocking. The twins had done a number on him. I stood for about five minutes before knocking again. It was a long shot to expect this nigga to open up.

"How you find out where I stay, bruh?" he asked through the door.

I sighed. "The niggas we used to play basketball with, bro. You aight? I was just coming by to check on you. I ain't heard from you in months, my nigga." A couple of minutes went by before hearing the locks unlatch. He peeked out, bat in hand, before stepping aside for me to come in. "Yo, you good, bro? Why you got shit boarded up?" I asked, looking around like I was confused before making eye contact with him.

"When's the last time you saw Nayeli?" he asked skeptically.

I sighed. "Shit. It's been a minute. We all moved out of the apartment, and she ain't been to the crib," I lied. He wasn't going to remember any of this shit, anyway.

He flopped down on the couch, pushing old food containers to the side. It was dark inside with the only light being from the one over the stove and the light emitting from the TV.

"Man, that girl got some evil shit going on with her. Something ain't right." My eyebrows scrunched as I inquired further. "She did something to me. Or them demonic ass babies did." My jaw tightened. "Sewed my lips closed without even touching me. That nigga probably did something to her ass. He had to, because how is she already pregnant by dude? She wouldn't have gone for that shit otherwise. I know that girl. I know that girl like the back of my hand," he rambled. He ain't know shit.

"Come on, bro, that sounds crazy as hell. What were the boards for? She doesn't know where you live, does she?" I entertained his suspicions.

He stood from his spot on the couch. "See, bruh, that's why I ain't told nobody about this shit. Ain't nobody going to believe me. What I got to lie about some crazy shit like that for?"

I sighed, irritated and wanting to go ahead and get this shit over with. I scooped a handful of sleeping powder from my pocket before blowing it into his face, and he instantly fell back on the couch.

I quickly began the process, wiping everything that happened after he woke up the morning of the Target incident until now. When done, I propped him on the couch in front of his game system, controller in hand. I snapped my fingers, and the boards on the windows disappeared, and I headed back to my car.

Hopefully, this was the last time we'd encounter Cameron, or at least, the last time I had to clean up their mess.

CHAPTER 18

SIMONE

I woke up in a great mood today because I was finally getting out of this fuckin house. Today was what was known in Mobile as Skinny Monday, a huge Mardi Gras celebration.

We hadn't participated in all the festivities during this Mardi Gras season. Nathan and Jessie had explained to us how the Salem Coven even used Mardi Gras floats to display their racial agenda. For that, our coven, along with many black people in the city, saved our fun to have in peace amongst each other.

After the first parade, we'd meet up with the rest of the coven in Africa Town to visit the older members of the coven and bring offerings to our ancestors in the nearby cemetery.

I just hung up a FaceTime call with Nayeli, who had been cooking breakfast. I looked over at Nathan still knocked out.

I nudged him. "Get up, bae! Nayeli is almost done cooking, and I'm hungry," I whined. I would have left his ass here, but he'd done something to the house so I couldn't jump.

He groaned as I climbed from the bed to head into the bathroom. When I returned, he was still in the same spot, hand tucked into his pajama pants. "At least take the fucking spell off the house so I can go by myself."

"Shut up, woman. I'm getting up." He sat up on the edge of the bed. "You ain't gone miss your first Mardi Gras, girl. Relax. It's only nine in the morning."

I rolled my eyes before walking into our closet. "Get your ass up and hurry up."

Prior to coming into my magic, I had no idea about all the festivities. Nayeli and I weren't allowed in Mobile, and Eva never brought us. So yeah, I was more excited than a little bit.

I slid into a comfortable all black matching set and a pair of red and black Air Max. I headed back into the bathroom to comb through my straightened hair and applied a second layer of lip gloss before heading downstairs, where Nathan awaited me.

"Uhh no. Turn that shit back off," I said, referring to the game.

He chuckled before standing. "You're rushing me to get up, and I'm ready before your slow ass."

I rolled my eyes while stuffing my things into my purse. He wrapped his arm around me and leaned in for a kiss as we jumped over to Nayeli and Jessie's house, which was five bedrooms and four and a half bathrooms. I didn't know what the hell Jessie had planned for my friend's reproductive organs.

"Eww! Don't nobody wanna see that shit." Jessie frowned, walking down the spiral staircase.

I rolled my eyes before parting with Nathan and going into the kitchen to join Nayeli. I inhaled.

"It smells good as hell in here," I expressed as my mouth watered. She smirked knowingly as I approached her, rubbing her huge belly. I was further along than she was, but she was showing more than me. "Hey, baby momma," I greeted as if we hadn't just gotten off the phone an hour ago.

The four of us sat around digging into our food over conversation, warnings, and threats. Nathan and Jessie had a long list of rules for us today.

"Rule number five, stay y'all motherfuckin ass where we can see you!" Nathan gritted as he eyed the both of us.

"But that was rule number one," Nayeli noted, rolling her eyes as she stuffed the spoonful of brown sugar oatmeal into her mouth.

"And it's rule number seven and ten, too. Stop interrupting and listen," Jessie scolded as she recoiled before throwing a grape at him from the fruit bowl sitting beside her plate. "For real, though, it better not be no shit today, or neither of you two motherfuckas will be making a move unless chauffeured by one of us."

"Okayyyy, we get it." I rolled my eyes. "Y'all tryna get y'all lil' daddy practice in, but y'all doing too much."

After eating, Nayeli was the only one left to get dressed, so we headed upstairs while they got on the game. I sat on the chaise in their bedroom as she showered and dressed. I looked up from my phone and noticed the distant look in her eye as she stared off into space.

"What's wrong with you?" I asked.

"Worried about Cameron," she whispered after peeking over at the bedroom door. I stilled as my eyes bucked slightly. She turned completely in my direction with her arms crossed over her chest. "What did you do, Simone?"

I looked away, breaking eye contact. "I told Nathan, but he took care of it and promised he wouldn't tell Jessie!"

She closed the bedroom door. "What the fuck, Simone? If Jessie tells me not to tell you something, what do you think I'ma do?"

"I know, but Cameron was Nathan's friend too at one point, and he doesn't want anything to happen to him, either so he won't say anything. I promise!" I knew she'd be mad, but I had faith in my baby.

She rolled her eyes, continuing to get dressed. "He better not!" she expressed, clearly annoyed.

I smiled brightly at the lively scene. Beautiful black people peacefully enjoying themselves whether over conversation or dancing to the music playing loudly throughout the streets. The turnout somewhat reminded me of what a homecoming tailgate looked like but bigger. We merged into the crowd of people walking up and down the streets awaiting the start of the first parade of the day.

"I can't believe we've been missing out on this our whole lives," I said to Nayeli, who walked beside me admiring the scene as well.

We walked up to a tent filled with tables and pans of food. A huge speaker stood up behind as people sat on the back of trucks digging into plates of various foods.

"Hey, baby," I heard Natalia's voice greet. "Y'all want something to eat?"

I looked around noticing the other women from the salon as well as some others from the coven.

"I just had breakfast, but I'll take a rib." My mouth watered in anticipation. Nathan chuckled, shaking his head at me. We enjoyed the festivities, swaying to the music as Nathan wrapped his arms tightly around me while slipping in and out of various conversations. Nayeli was off to the side sitting in Jessie's lap eating a plate of barbeque. Suddenly, police sirens could be heard nearing as I slightly panicked. That was never a good sign, especially on a street filled with hundreds of black people.

"Chill, baby. That means the parade is about to start," Nathan informed me as I noticed people moving closer to the street.

"Now these sneaky motherfuckas wanna be paranoid." Jessie chuckled, and Nathan joined in.

The parade was nothing like I'd ever seen before. Big, beautifully decorated floats filled with already drunk float riders tossing snack cakes, teddy bears, and other random things to the attendees. High school and local marching bands stomped through, playing latest hits between each float while the dance girls flawlessly performed eight counts. People were riding horseback. There was luxurious convertible cars with crowned women waving from the back of them. It was a whole vibe.

I felt so uncultured out here, having missed this in the previous years. By the time it was all over, Nathan had arms filled with teddy bears and boxes of snack cakes. Everyone quickly packed the tent and food into the R.V. to move to the next location. While they headed over to set up, we headed to Africa town to Nathan's grandma's house for a little.

The small settlement was surrounded by tall, thick trees. It appeared a bit run down, but I could tell it was lively and magical in its day. This was where all the witches and warlocks of our coven had started and hailed from. The history behind it alone was crazy.

The small forgotten town was the destination of the last slaves brought over into the country through Mobile Bay, having no idea they'd brought over a ship full of powerful African hoodoo specialists. Once they'd regained their strength and dignity, torture wasn't even a strong enough word to describe what these slave traders had endured at the hands of my ancestors.

As soon as we pulled into the yard, I got out to breathe in the welcoming air. The tension I carried around in my body unconsciously quickly eased. I felt safe and unbothered amongst these trees.

We followed Nathan up the porch steps and into the old worn house identical to the one in the Ancestral Plain. We weren't going to be here long. Tally had him getting some old pictures together for his dad's birthday celebration approaching.

After leaving the bathroom, I walked past Jessie and Nayeli sucking each other's faces off, and I frowned. I stood in the screen door surveying the neighborhood. Suddenly, my features scrunched.

"What is it?" Nayeli asked, pulling away from Jessie.

"It's those two kids again. What are they doing over here?" I asked. If you didn't know of this place's existence, you wouldn't be able to find it, so how?

The four of us stood in the doorway watching them dip off behind a house, looking through the windows.

"What are they up to?" Nathan questioned aloud. "That's your grandma's house, Simone," he informed me as I looked back to him swiftly. Why hadn't anyone told me about this house before now?

I turned back, staring out at them, before Nayeli cut her eye at me, already knowing what I was thinking, literally.

"Nathannn," I whined.

"Y'all two are fuckin killing me, bruh. A nigga just wanna enjoy Mardi Gras, not go on a fuckin witch hunt. Come on!" he expressed, and I ignored his rant and exited the house, creeping up on them.

Coming through the neighbor's backyard, we saw them peeping through the windows before walking through the wall. We tiptoed up the back porch as I wondered how we'd get in. I didn't have a key. As if reading my mind, Nathan spoke. "Marie used the same blood magic on the house as she did the cabin, so just press your finger into the keyhole."

Doing as instructed, I heard the lock pop after pulling back a bloody finger. As soon as we made eye contact, they tried to take off. Jessie and Nathan quickly grabbed them. "Where y'all lil' motherfuckas think y'all going? Y'all ain't slipping away again."

"What y'all doing here?" I asked as they struggled to get out of Jessie and Nathan's hold. "Calm down. We're not going to do anything to you," I informed them, and they surprisingly settled.

They explained to us in some form of broken English that they had been forced out of their homes on the islands off the coast of Georgia and the Carolinas due to gentrification. This was the safest place they could think to migrate to because they claimed to have family right over here in Africa town.

That explained why they were around here doing magic carelessly. They hailed from an island where on part of it everyone on it possessed the same gifts. They were scavenging and stealing food to feed their people. Silence fell over the room as we looked from one another.

"Things are different here in the city than on the islands. Everyone here doesn't have the same gifts as us, and everybody that does doesn't always have the best intentions. It's best to be as discreet as possible," I informed the duo.

They looked at one another before speaking. "Come back with us and help my ma find our family in town?" the boy asked.

I looked back at Nathan who sighed in irritation.

"Baby, they're kids, and these people need our help. Clearly there is a language barrier, but I can understand them."

He grunted, leading the way out of the back door before locking up. We rode in silence for a while as Nayeli and Jessie trailed us in his car back to the abandoned warehouse behind her restaurant. I turned in my seat toward them. "Why were you in that house today?"

"My ma say das wea our family is," the girl said. Nathan and I made eye contact before he sighed, and I turned back in my seat. Shit just kept getting crazier. I guess we'd have to bring offerings to the ancestors another time.

We got out and walked over to the same spot we'd seen them at previously.

Are you sure about this, Simone? Nayeli asked telepathically, scaring the shit out of me.

Yes, and don't do that shit again, I responded, rolling my eyes before walking through the wall behind the duo as the other three trailed behind. Everyone inside stood and took several steps back at the sight of us.

"Zaire? Zara? What were you thinking bringing these people here?" a woman, who seemed to be their leader, asked in very clear English. She was beautiful with smooth dark skin and long, thick locs hanging down to her lower back.

Suddenly, the thoughts of everyone in the room flooded my head. My hands went up to either side of my face as I keeled over.

"Please stop!" I screamed.

"What's wrong, baby? What the fuck are y'all doing to her?" Nathan gritted toward the crowd of frightened people.

"Too many voices. Too many thoughts. I can't control it," I forced out. It was driving me crazy.

The leader inched toward me slowly before lifting my head up and staring into my eyes as the voices settled. Her eyes watered as she looked at me.

"Marie Dupree?" she questioned with a shaky voice.

CHAPTER 19

NAYELI

I STOOD BACK UP against the wall in Jessie's arms watching the exchange in confusion. The beautiful dark-skinned woman caressed Simone's face as she calmed.

"Marie Dupree?" she asked. "Well, obviously you're not her, but you have to be a close relative. You have her face," she choked out with a light chuckle.

"I'm her granddaughter. Is that who they were looking for?" she asked, referring to the twins, who I learned names were Zaire and Zara.

She nodded. "Yes. Where is she? I haven't been able to feel her presence since I got here. I've been trying not to think the worst."

I sighed. We were going to be here for a while. What were the odds of Simone being related to the kids we'd been chasing down for quite some time, let alone a whole coven?

We'd been here for about forty-five minutes, standing back while Simone talked with her newfound family members, when Jessie stepped out to take a call about one of his properties. As soon as the door closed behind him, I hurriedly pulled Nathan away from Simone.

"Thanks for taking care of the Cameron thing. You're not gonna tell Jessie, right? I don't want anything to happen to Cameron."

"I got you. I don't want nothing to happen to him, either so I ain't gonna tell him." He smirked before continuing. "The twins did a number on his ass, though. Nigga had his crib boarded up hiding from your ass."

I sighed, returning to my spot before Jessie returned. I felt sorry for him. He endured so much in a short time and really had no idea what was going on with him or around him. He wrapped his arm around me, palming my belly and bringing me out of my thoughts.

"We don't have a place to call home anymore. Marie was all we had outside of the islands. Everyone else descended from any parts of our coven was still on the island, and this is what's left of us," the woman spoke. "Without family, I don't know where else to turn. We don't know anything about how these cities operated. My people are not accustomed to the hustle and bustle of these cities."

"Like I said, I am Marie's granddaughter, so you do still have family here. Let me speak to the leader of our coven and see how we can help. In the meantime, you guys have to be more discreet," she stressed.

After getting them set up with some food for now, we went to catch the last parade of the night. That was another two hours we were out enjoying the vibe and unlimited food. By the time I started to feel drowsy, Ms. Felicia was fixing our to-go-plates.

I loved my mother-in-law. We had a lot in common, and she was always looking out for me for whatever I needed. Cameron's mom seemed to like me sometimes, but she acted very nonchalant when we were around one another, so I didn't know, but I definitely didn't get the same vibe from Ms. Felicia that I got from her.

Today had definitely been an interesting one. We rarely had days that weren't. A quick stop had turned into an all-day quest. The development of the new coven in town was a twist none of us expected. We were now headed home. Thank God for those to-go plates she fixed us because I was tired as hell, and cooking was the last thing on my agenda tonight.

I curled up comfortably on the couch watching TV and eating from my plate. Jessie appeared beside me shirtless and lay in my lap, facing my belly.

"How did you like your first Mardi Gras experience?" he inquired with his eyes closed.

"It was fun. I hate that we've been missing out on it, but at least the twins won't." Seeing the excitement in all the kids scattered around enjoying the fun and festivities was the highlight of the day. I couldn't wait to experience those moments with them.

He smirked and lifted my shirt, kissing it as the twins reacted to him. "What do you think they are?" he asked as they continued to interact with each other. We were going to our gender appointment tomorrow.

I rolled my eyes as I continued to chew the combination of macaroni and baked beans that was stuffed in my jaws. He always wanted to talk to me when my mouth was busy.

"I hope girls," I answered before biting into my rib.

He laughed. "Hurry up, baby, so we can go to sleep."

His freaky ass said while rubbing my back. I never needed attention from him because he damn near smothered me at all times, but I liked that shit, though. This pregnancy just made me easily irritated with everything.

I moved my plate aside and looked down at him. "We're going to sleep for real, Jessie. I'm tired."

"Chill out, baby. I'ma do all the work." He smiled before kissing it again. He was so fine. I loved my chocolate nigga. "All you gotta do is cum, baby."

"All I wanna do is eat this food and watch this show," I whined. I was always down for a good fuck session, but this day had exhausted me completely. The twins had finally calmed, and I just wanted to rest.

"Aight, I'ma leave you alone, but tomorrow, I'ma tear that ass up," he said before nuzzling his head close into my lap and closing his eyes. "Wake me up when you're ready to get in the bed."

⚜

"Hurry up!" I whined to Jessie. It was the next morning, and usually, it took me longer to get ready, but this nigga was moving like we weren't headed to find out important news.

He descended the spiral staircase pulling his shirt over his head, smirking. "Baby, we're not running late, and no matter how early we get there, the appointment time is still the same."

"Whateva, nigga, bring your ass on!" I replied. He was so annoying. No one asked him all that. He just needed to do what I said, simple. He had a whole temper tantrum when he thought I didn't want to have his babies, and now he was acting like it was no big deal.

"Aye, don't get beside yourself. Do I need to remind you before we leave who runs this motherfuckin show, and why it's me?" Jessie asked with flared nostrils, trying to appear serious but I was amused.

I pushed him toward the door. "When we get back, I'll show you why it's me!"

"I can't wait." He winked at me before pulling my car door open and closing it behind me before rounding the car and getting in. We took the twenty five minute drive to the doctor's office in silence as he nodded to the music blasting through the stereo system, and I scoured Pinterst and Tik Tok for ideas and themes for my restaurant.

Thankfully, it hadn't been packed in here as usual and I hoped I wouldn't be in here as long as I usually was. I hated that about doctors' offices and hospitals. The wait was always the most dreadful part.

I sat beside him in the waiting room scrolling through my

phone as he rubbed my stomach, calming the twins because they'd been on one this morning.

"You never told me what you wanted them to be," I said, looking over the side of his handsome, lightly bearded face. His face was structured perfectly as I picked a piece of lint from his beard. Either way, our babies were going to be gorgeous.

"I'm fine with whatever we get, baby." He kissed me before turning back into the basketball highlights on his phone. My eyebrows dipped as I stared at the side of his face. He peeked out the corner of his eye before turning to me. "What?"

"You already know, don't you?" I asked knowingly as he smirked, and I huffed. "How long have you known, Jessie? That's not fair." I pouted. We were supposed to find out together.

"Nine years."

Damn. What hadn't their grandma showed them?

"Ms. Edwards?" the nurse called, drawing my attention away from him as we stood and followed her to the back. She left us to return with the doctor.

"Stop pouting." He approached me as I stood beside the examination table, arms crossed above my belly.

"What else did she show you? I want to know everything."

"No, you don't, and I'm not telling you." He lifted me onto the table. "Just know we're going to be happy, and so are *all* of our kids."

Knock, knock. My eyes bucked before I could respond.

"Good morning, Ms. Edwards and dad," the doctor greeted as Jessie took a step back smirking at the turmoil on my face. "How are the twins?"

I cleared my throat. "They're fine. Recently discovered they don't like garlic, so there's that," I responded, scooting backward on the table. Just the smell alone would have me throwing up the contents of my stomach.

I lifted my shirt as I watched them prepare for the ultrasound, and Jessie moved closer. I cut my eye at him. Why'd he even care? He already knew. I was salty as hell about that. I jerked at the cold gel spread on the bottom of my belly. My eyes were glued to the monitor as the double heartbeats rang throughout the small room.

"Okay. Baby A is." She paused as I waited anxiously. "A boy, and baby B." She paused again as I looked over at a smirking Jessie.

"A girl," he finished as my gaze swung back at the monitor at the 3D images. Jessie wiped the tears I hadn't even known were falling. Wow, a boy and a girl. My doctor printed the 3D ultrasound images off before handing them over to me and confirming I didn't have any questions, comments, or concerns. The nurse scheduled my next appointment and sent us on our way. I sat in the passenger seat as an amazed Jessie stared at the ultrasound pictures.

"How many more times am I doing this, Jessie?" I finally asked. I needed to know what *all our kids* meant. I wasn't sure how many times my little body could carry sets of twins.

"You don't need to know that, baby. Just sit back and enjoy life."

I snatched the ultrasound from his hands. "Take me to my restaurant," I ordered as he obliged.

I was having a lunch date with my mom and Felicia. This would be the first time his mom had tasted my cooking, and I was a bit nervous. I'd come by to prep yesterday, so all I had to do was slide it in the oven.

"Can I stay?" he asked, parking in front of my restaurant.

"No!" I replied simply as I got out and slammed the door.

"I love you too, baby!" he replied while laughing. He thought shit was so damn funny.

Once inside, I turned on the music before dropping my things off in the back office and washing my hands. I propped my phone up to FaceTime Simone while I removed the pans from the fridge.

"Girl! Fix your face. What's your problem already? They aren't girls?" She scoffed as she picked up.

"Jessie's ass already knew what they were. He knew this whole time and didn't tell me," I responded, sliding the pan of marinated chicken and three cheese macaroni into the oven.

"Stop pouting. You would have been mad if he would have ruined it for you. What are they?"

I rolled my eyes away from her. "A boy and a girl," I answered before putting my cabbage on. It wouldn't take long to cook at all. They'd instructed me to cook whatever I was craving, and I couldn't wait to tear into this food.

"Yay!" She smiled brightly. "You got your boy and your girl. You can be done." She laughed.

"Not likely. He did let it slip that we weren't done having kids, but he won't tell me how many more times. How many more times can I do this? Carrying two babies? This shit is exhausting. How does he get a glimpse into the future, and I don't?"

"Are you done pouting? You're worrying about shit that's going to happen years from now." I rolled my eyes again. "What are you cooking? It doesn't even matter. I'm on the way!" she announced before hanging up.

The threesome arrived at the same time, and they all greeted me with warm embraces. I'd only known Ms. Cross for a little while, but it was like we'd known one another for years.

"What are we having? It's killing me," she asked.

"I'll tell you when we sit down to eat," I said, and she pouted. "Go ahead and get seated. I'm about to bring it out now," I finished as Simone followed me to the kitchen. We quickly returned with the food, and Simone grabbed the pitcher of fresh sweet tea from the bar.

"Nayeli, stop playing with me!" my mom said as I was about to put my first forkful in my mouth. I smiled and pulled the ultrasound from my pocket and placed it in the middle of our table. "A boy and a girl."

They gasped simultaneously while taking in the images.

"I'm about to be a grandma!" my mom said as she teared up.

"Yeah, of plenty, apparently," I said sarcastically before Simone laughed, choking on the sip of tea she'd just taken while my mom and Ms. Cross gave confused stares. I sighed. "Jessie already knew what they were, and he knows how many children we're going to have, and he won't tell me." I pouted again, hoping his mom would make him tell me what I wanted to know before stuffing my cheeks. I was starving.

"Yeah, a quick glimpse into the future is my mom's special birthday gift to her grands when they turn sixteen. You don't need to know that, baby girl. Just enjoy what life has in store for you." I rolled my eyes away. Like mother, like son. He said the same thing earlier. "Oh, and I love the marinade on this chicken!"

I smiled. I couldn't wait to get my restaurant up and running. Feeding everyone in the port city and surrounding areas!

CHAPTER 20

GABBY

I FINALLY HAD my friends back, and it felt great. Eva took a little more time to come around than Tally, and it was understandable. I hurt her, but we were better now.

The three of us sat around the living room sipping from our wine glasses over conversation. We agreed to meet up like this once a week. We had a lot of catching up to do. Well, with them. There was nothing much to really talk about with me. My life had been stagnant for some time now. Nothing had changed. Hell, I hadn't even aged. Still nineteen years old. My own daughter had surpassed me.

"Honestly, did you expect anything less?" Tally asked. "He loves you, Gabby, and he wants you back with him and Simone."

I rolled my eyes at what I knew to be the truth. I just informed them of my current frustrations with Chase. I already had it out with him, too. Dragging my baby down a dead-end road with him. He'd already known how this could consume someone, and I was pissed he roped her into it. I wanted her to live and enjoy her life, not waste it trying to bring me back when we already knew it wasn't possible.

Before I could respond, I was interrupted by a presence and looked over to find a waddling Simone. I instantly smiled at the glowing sight of my daughter and granddaughter. Her glow was brighter every time I saw her. I loved seeing her.

"Hey, Ma, hey Ma, hey, Tally," she greeted as she came to take a seat between Eva and myself.

"Hey, baby. What are you doing over here?" Eva asked her while caressing her protruding belly. They'd done a great job with her. Both Eva and Tally. I honestly had no idea how things would turn out after I was gone. I didn't know if she'd actually make it out of that church at all, let alone alive. I was forever grateful for my prying friends.

"It's actually a good thing you guys are all here. Those new witches in town, we ran into them again," she responded, looking over at me. "We met the rest of them. Talked to them about where they came from, and why they're here," she continued to stare at me. "You knew who they were the last time I brought them up, didn't you?"

My eyes bucked slightly. "I wasn't sure." I sighed as Eva and Tally shared a confused expression. Thankfully, this wasn't something that could be held over my head.

"So? Who are they then?" Tally asked. As the current leader of our coven, she was ultimately responsible for the prolonging of the coven. Of every member's wellbeing.

"Family, apparently. We caught them sneaking into my grandma's house. Thanks for telling me about that, by the way," she added sarcastically as I sighed. I didn't even know the house was still standing. "They came from the islands on the coast of the Carolinas, pushed out by gentrification. They've never been off those islands, so they didn't know that they needed to be discreet. This was the only place they knew to come because they have family. Their leader says I look just like Marie."

I teared up a bit. She did. She looked just like my mom, more like her than me. Tally and Eva began to flicker. Their candles were burning out. Two hours was never enough time.

"Come see me when you get back," Tally stated before they disappeared, leaving me alone under the scrutinizing eyes of my daughter, who in appearance alone, was the older one in the room.

"What is it?" Simone asked, looking down at her hands. "Do I seem fragile? Do you not think I can handle certain things? Because after all this time, you and Nathan can't seem to tell me everything, both claiming there weren't any more secrets."

I sighed again, wiping her tears away. This baby had been doing a number on her emotions. I could hear the angry tremble in her voice, but the tears were sad ones.

"Nobody's keeping secrets, Simone. I didn't know the house was still standing or if another family moved in. It was unoccupied for two decades, Simone, and about your cousins, I told you I wasn't sure." I pulled her into my chest and smoothed her hair back. "We're not trying to hurt you or keep anything from you, just protect you, and can you honestly say you haven't been moving recklessly?"

She pulled away to look up at me. "Nathan's been over here running his mouth?" she asked, annoyed and jealous.

"He is my godson. He can come visit me whenever, especially when he's venting about your hardheaded ass."

She pulled away, wiping her eyes and quickly changing the subject, not enjoying being in the hot seat. "What am I supposed to do? I can't just leave them to continue to struggle in that warehouse. They don't have food, and they have babies with them. Newborn babies."

I smiled. Her heart was so pure. She was going to be a great leader someday. "How does home look? Are any of the coven members living over there?"

"That was my first time going. Looks pretty much abandoned. All except the cemetery. It looks pretty festive."

"Get Tally to call a meeting with the other members and

present the idea of moving them to Africa town in the abandoned homes, but you have to get their okay first. Even though they are abandoned, they still have owners. They could probably bring it back to life. I'd never met them, but my mom talked about them all the time. She visited the islands when she was a little girl. She said they were all great gardeners and very spiritual," I advised.

"What about any other family? Do we have any?"

I sighed. "The witch's war in the eighties killed off a lot of us. On both sides, actually. That is what ultimately helped us come to a truce."

⁕

"Wake up, baby!" I heard before my eyes fluttered open and landed on the top of Chase's head as he left kisses around my neck. After Simone left, I did some cleaning before showering and taking it in for the night. "Gabrielle, wake up, baby!" he whispered without looking up.

"Get off me, Chase." I pushed his head away before turning over to the other side. I was still mad about him getting Simone involved in messing with necromancy, especially while she was pregnant.

"Stop acting like that, baby. I haven't seen you in three days." He left more kisses on the nape of my neck.

"Yeah, well, it was twenty-one years before that. You'll live," I retorted.

He paused before pulling away and flipping me over. He stared down at me. "Was that shit my fault?"

Yes. It was, I thought. Had he not followed me that day they wouldn't have found me there, and my plan to flee would have worked, but I wouldn't bring that up. I longed for my night to remain peaceful, so we just stared blankly at one another before he leaned down to kiss me again.

"Stop acting like that," he said before leaving a trail of kisses down the front of my body. He pulled my shorts down, leaving gentle kisses on my middle. "You don't miss this?" he asked as I gasped.

He had no idea how much I did. His reemergence had been months ago, and we'd yet to have sex because we couldn't stop arguing long enough to make it to that part of the short two hour visit. Whether it was me blaming him for getting me killed or him blaming me for trying to leave. It never failed. In the last five minutes, we'd calm down and find love again, but not soon enough for us to enjoy any form of pleasure from one another; which was probably why he chose to come so late this time. If I was already in bed, there would be no time for arguments.

I spent countless nights digging into myself with him in mind. My fiancé, the white boy who came into my life and destroyed all stereotypes I thought of him. His lips were full and soft. He always smelled edible. He wasn't white boy crazy, just Gabby crazy, and his dick, whew! *My dick,* I thought as I felt it poking into my calf as he sucked on my swollen bud. My body convulsed from the unending pleasure as he kissed his way back up that same trail and entered me slowly as I winced from the pain. Nothing but fingers had been in there for the past two decades.

"I was supposed to be putting babies in here every nine months," he groaned in my ear as I moaned into his. His hands left my breasts and moved down to grip my ass before digging deeper.

"Chase!" I whined as a chill shot through my body. Hell, I had no idea how much I had missed this need. My arms tightened around his neck, alerting him that I was close to my peak. He took one of my nipples into his mouth while delivering lethal strokes.

"Fuckk!" he dragged, releasing inside of me and lying on my chest as my body relaxed underneath his. We lay in that position basking in our sexual highs with the little time we had left together. "I love you, Gabrielle," he said before leaving another kiss on my chest and getting up, heading to the bathroom.

I wasn't ready for him to go. This was one of the main reasons I didn't want him coming over here all the time. I knew I'd start to want more time, and that wasn't possible. He returned and pulled his pants up over his waist before reaching into his pocket and taking a seat on the bed beside me. He grabbed my left hand and slid my ring back down onto my ring finger. "If you take this off again, we're going to have a problem, Gabrielle."

I loved that he was the only person who called me Gabrielle. Never Gabby.

CHAPTER 21

SIMONE

I woke up today in a great mood. I hadn't had any morning sickness, and Tally had made Nathan take me off house arrest. I met up with the other members, and they agreed to letting the new coven live on the vacant properties until they could get their own built. There was plenty of available land and plenty of trees that could be cut down if needed.

I was going to meet with them to give them the news a little later. Right now, I was getting my little girl's room together while Nathan slept. We decided to name her Naomi. She had been getting so big. I woke up this morning feeling just as big as Nayeli.

My little girl was all I thought about these days, especially when he had me locked up in this house. Her and bringing my mom back. I knew I told her I'd leave it alone, but I couldn't. I felt like I was getting close. I'd just be careful not to document anything else in my spell book, and she wouldn't find out.

I was going to meet up with my dad later, too. She had been giving him hell since finding out we were working together. He should have warned me not to mention it to her. *She'd just have to get over it,* I thought as I continued to fold t-shirts and blankets I'd just gotten from the dryer. I rolled my eyes at the sound of the toilet flushing in our bedroom. He'd been walking around with an attitude because he ain't want me to be from under his thumb yet. He peeked in at me before heading downstairs to get on the game.

After throwing a quick breakfast together, I headed upstairs to get dressed to head out. He was still pouting about me leaving. He talked all that big shit about authority and got overruled by his momma. I slid into a gray jogger set and some all white Air Force Ones. It wasn't too cold out anymore, but it wasn't by any means warm yet. I let my hair hang below my shoulders before giving myself a once over in the body length mirror in our bedroom. I'd gotten so big that it was starting to become uncomfortable.

I descended the stairs to find him in his same spot in the living room on the couch with his headset on, controller in hand, and a plate of the food I whipped up for breakfast sitting on the table in front of him.

I rounded the table and took a seat on his lap. "I'm about to go, bae," I let him know while stroking his beard. He started letting it grow out and was looking like somebody's fine ass daddy. "Give me a kiss," I demanded, puckering my lips. He cut his eye at me before giving me his cheek to kiss.

I burst out laughing before cupping his face in between one hand and turning him back toward me. "You don't even have a reason to be mad, so stop acting like a baby. There's only room in this house for one of those. Now, give me a fuckin' kiss." Deciding not to wait for him to have me fucked up again, I pulled his face closer to mine before sucking his bottom lip into my mouth and circling my tongue with is as he did the same, and his free hand gripped around my waist. I pulled away to leave one last peck. "Be back in a little. Love you."

He stared at me with his mouth agape. "Wow, Simone. Hurry and bring your ass back home!" he said to my back as I made my exit.

. . .

I pulled up in front of Nayeli's restaurant in no time. She'd been there preparing for her grand opening soon. I walked in to find her bodyguard, Jessie, leaning back into one of the booths watching a game on the flatscreens hanging from the walls and eating one of the entrées from the finalized menu.

"Yeah, bro. She just walked in," Jessie said into the phone nuzzled between his ear and shoulder.

"Y'all are pathetic as fuck," I expressed to him before rolling my eyes and heading to the back to find Nayeli. She sat in her office examining her employee uniforms as her back massager buzzed through the room. My niece and nephew were giving her ass the blues. "I see your warden is still on your neck."

Startled a bit, she looked at me before laughing. Unlike Tally, Eva nor Felicia hadn't taken her side and encouraged his hovering. Like we were just out here doing super reckless shit. "I don't even pay his ass any mind as long as he stays his ass up there and not getting on my nerves unless he is hungry."

I stayed to chat for a little while before heading out back to the warehouse. I walked through the side entrance to find the large group spread out doing various things. Some meditating, some tending to the young, the old, and some rationing food.

"Simone!" Giselle, their leader and my cousin, greeted from beside me. She approached smiling as the familial connection was now evident. Both she and the twins, who were also my cousins, favored my mom.

She informed me that although my Gran was a lot older than her, she was her favorite cousin. She'd go visit the islands every summer to hang with Giselle and her older sisters.

"I have good news!" I informed as she stood in front of me. "The other coven members have agreed to let you guys live in the vacant homes in Africa town until you guys can get settled in your own homes."

There was plenty of land to build on and a large gardening area.

She smiled as relief shone in her eyes. "I don't know how to thank you, Simone."

"Don't worry about it. We're family. I've never really had an extended family, so I'm happy to help."

She smiled brightly before going to gather everyone to move. After gathering their belongings, they all made themselves invisible and moved toward their new home, where they'd be safe and free to roam and practice. I stopped through the restaurant to let Nayeli know I was out. I walked back through the dining area.

"Be sure to tell your boy I'm headed out." I rolled my eyes away from Jessie as I exited the building and slid into my car.

In no time, I was driving down the long street surrounded by huge, full trees. The seclusion of this small, wooded community was perfect for them to move around as they did back on the island.

I pulled in front of my grandma's cottage styled home in Africa town as the coven went through picking houses based on family size. I got out and met Giselle, Ziarre, and Zara on the front porch. This was obviously where they were going to be staying.

Using her finger, the door's lock popped, and we entered the home. I looked around the living room area at the pictures hung up all over of my mom, grandma, and grandpa. I quickly gave myself a tour of the home. I didn't really get a chance to look around when we followed the twins inside a couple of days ago. I ventured down the hallway to what was my mom's room.

I went in, picking up a picture of the two of them. Seemed they had a great relationship with one another. I wished I could have gotten to know the both of them the right way.

"You never met her?" Giselle asked from the doorway, startling me.

I shook my head. "She died before I was born. My mom said she spent most of her pregnancy trying to bring her back, but it wasn't successful. The spells only kept knocking her out, and now my mom is trying to make me stop looking for a way to bring her back." I sighed.

She frowned, entering the room. "How did she die? Marie? I never did ask, but necromancy only works if the deceased died from supernatural causes." My gaze shot up in her direction. "And even then, it takes a really strong spell and a large amount of power to complete the process successfully."

"Cancer. She had cancer," I informed, placing the picture back into its previous spot. "So, wait. There is a way to bring my mom back?" I asked as my heart pounded in my chest, trying not to get my hopes up before I received an answer.

"Yes." She smiled as she nodded. "I could help you with it." She looked over at the corner of the room, smiling wider. "Our coven has a strong connection to the spirit world. Come!" she instructed, holding both hands out at her sides.

Reluctantly, I moved in her direction, grabbing her hand and watching the woman from the pictures appear across from me holding her other hand. I gasped as her free hand went up to caress my cheek, and she smiled.

"Simone." She wiped the lone tear from my face. "I'm so proud of you," she added, wiping the other away.

"Grandma?" I jerked as the tears continued.

"Shhh!" She caressed my belly, smiling wider. "We're going to have plenty more interactions from now on." She looked over at Giselle for reassurance as she nodded in return.

I had so many questions I wanted to ask her. So much I wanted to tell her about her life, my life, my mom's life, how to excel at this witch shit. I felt she had the answers to all my questions. I longed for a grandmother who actually loved me. That was one connection I'd yet to feel. My emotions were running rapidly as we continued to stare at one another.

"How are you here?" I questioned as I continued to stare, taking in the uncanny resemblance between us.

"I'm always lurking around here checking on my house, you just can't see me, but Giselle here can see all of us over here." She smiled. "You got strength and resilience in your blood. You will become a very powerful witch in time and a great leader one day." I frowned with my head cocked. *A leader? A leader to who?* She caressed my face again. "I know you have a lot of questions. Once everything and everyone is settled, we'll talk." Smiled again before disappearing into thin air, and I was left speechless.

I sat in my car getting myself together from the emotional roller coaster I'd taken myself on during the drive over. I was meeting my dad at the apartment he shared with Chasity, but he hadn't made it back yet.

I just met my grandma for the first time, and the resemblance between us was crazy. Only difference being a couple of shades. I couldn't wait to go back to visit my mom and tell her what I learned. There was no way I was letting it go now. I saw my dad's pickup truck back into a spot across from me and climbed from my car.

He approached me smiling just as big as he always had every time he saw me, carrying a bag of food in his hands. Thank God because I was starving.

We sat and talked over lunch before starting our meditation session. We'd been doing these every now and again to help me control everybody's thoughts and voices, so I'd be able to only hear them when I wanted to and wouldn't have to worry about being swarmed by them all the time. I enjoyed this time, though, because meditating with my dad also helped calm me. I wasn't as easily angered and agitated as I'd been before or earlier in my pregnancy.

When we were done, I updated him on everything I'd been doing with the Gullah coven. I'd also given him the information Giselle had given me about Necromancy. I'd gotten full and lazy after eating and meditating as I sat back up against the couch with my feet up.

"This is good news, baby girl. Honestly, I started to get discouraged, but at least now we knew why it didn't work for her all those years ago. She's coming home," he choked, caressing my cheek before we jolted forward into a vision.

I lay back as my mom and dad stood beside my bed cradling my little girl.

"She's so beautiful, Simone," my mom said to me as I returned an exhausted smile, and she swiped at her river of tears with my dad comforting her emotion with a hand to her back.

I gasped, finding myself back on the couch as my dad and I shared a shocked gaze.

"Did you see that too?" he asked.

That had been my first future vision. "Yeah. Mom's coming back before I give birth!"

CHAPTER 22

NATHAN

I SAT on top of the counter between the Jack and Jill sinks in our en suite bathroom listening to Simone as she straightened her hair and told me everything that had happened with her and her cousin, Giselle. There hadn't been an uneventful day in our lives since she'd come into her magic.

In a matter of days, she repopulated Africa town and gave a coven housing and access to food. I admired how she stepped into her role as a witch so easily, like she'd known about this part of her for her whole life.

"She said the reason it didn't work was because her death wasn't supernatural and that she could help me bring my mom back." My eyes bucked in surprise. She put the flat iron down and turned toward me. "And I met my grandma, too." My eyebrows dropped in confusion as she continued. "Giselle is some kind of anchor for the dead. I held her hand, and she just appeared right in front of me. The resemblance in us is crazy, bae."

A subtle smile stretched across my face as I continued to admire the mother of my child. That looming sense of sadness hovering over her had disappeared completely. Before her twenty-first birthday, she'd always had a distant sadness in her eyes. I hated seeing her like that, but I couldn't tell her about what she wouldn't understand.

She went from foster care to being adopted by her best friend's mom, only to find out years later that she was actually her godmother. To now have both of her parents in her life, extraordinary abilities, and our own baby on the way.

I couldn't wait to meet my princess. I could already picture her pretty little face and the attitude that came along with it, courtesy of her mom.

"So, what's the plan?" I asked reluctantly. Her hardheaded ass ain't listen to nobody. I knew for a fact that Gabby had shut this shit down, and here she was still moving forward.

"Why, so you can snitch?" she asked, staring at me through the mirror. "Well, don't bother because I'm gonna tell her myself before we're ready."

I guess Gabby had let it slip that I'd been visiting and venting.

"What's the plan?" I growled. Fuck all that shit she was talking. I wanted to know how strenuous this shit would be on her body. On my baby.

She rolled them damn eyes again. "We're going to try in a couple of months to give them time to settle and build their strength back up. They have a spell. It's just gonna take me, my dad, and at least ten of their elders including Giselle."

"What are you gonna have to do?"

She sighed. "I don't know yet. Stop worrying. I'm going to be fine, and so is she."

I looked down at her protruding belly. She finished with her hair and getting dressed to meet up with my mom, Eva, Nayeli, and Ms. Felicia to shop for the babies.

"Aight, bae, I'll be back in a little. Love you!" she said, descending the stairs and leaving a kiss on my lips while I focused on the game I was in the middle of.

"Aight, bae. I love you, too."

I'd gone into the kitchen to grab something to drink before returning to my spot on the living room couch as all the information Simone had given me swarmed my thoughts. I'd never had an interest in Necromancy because I'd always been taught it was dangerous to play with the dead, but now, the interest was strong. I'd give anything to have my dad back. I wondered if they could help me, too.

I looked over at the time and decided to go visit my mom to see how she felt about it. I was sure she wanted her husband back, too, and if there was a way, then why not? Grabbing my phone, I quickly jumped to her house before she left to meet up with them at the mall.

"Maaa!" I yelled as soon as I landed in the living room. I walked through the kitchen as she came in from the back of the house searching her purse for something before looking up at me.

"What, boy? You know I'm supposed to meet Simone and them soon."

"You know about the plan to bring Gabby back?"

"Not really. I don't know any details, just that they plan to try, and it might work this time. Why? Nobody's going to let anything happen to her, Nathan."

"Nah, it's not that." I paused before going to lean up against the counter. "Do you think it will work for dad? Could they help bring him back, too?"

She sighed, walking toward me. "I'm not sure, son. There was a lot done to him. I'm not sure he'd even want to try. He wouldn't be the same. Those torturous memories would come back with him. Why don't you go ask him about it?" she said before kissing my cheek. "I'm about to go to the mall. Call me if you need me."

I sighed before going up to my bedroom to go visit my dad. My room still looked the same as it did before. It was still black and red themed. All my football trophies remained in their same spot. I smiled faintly looking at the father-son first place track trophy as the memory played out in my head.

15 years ago

I stood on the grass off to the side sweating bullets. My dad and I had made it through the first two rounds and were about to start the last race. He looked back at me, and his eyebrows dropped.

"What's wrong with you, boy?" he asked.

This was the annual father-son track tournament in Africa town. This was my first time running, and although we'd run the first two rounds, this last duo had been dusting niggas all day.

"I'm a lil' nervous," I responded. My dad had been an all-state track champion in high school, and I didn't want to be the reason we didn't win it all today.

"What are you nervous for? We just won two. We only got one more, then we can go grub. Shake that shit off, you got this." He nudged me to the side as I took a deep breath.

He went over to kneel in front of the post before the shot was fired, and he took off, sprinting around the track as if it was as easy as breathing.

I took another deep breath as I positioned myself. As soon as the baton touched my hand, I bolted. I could feel the wind whipping past my face and hear the crowd cheering me on. I sped up, nearing the finish line. As soon as I slowed down my dad lifted me into the air.

"Told you, you had it!" He smiled.

That'd been my favorite memory with my dad and the last good one because he'd been killed a couple of months later. I sighed, pulling the candle from the top drawer and taking my place on the floor before removing the pocketknife from my pocket.

As soon as I appeared in the living room, I sprinted up the staircase. As usual, he was engrossed in the video game before he looked at me.

"What's up, son? Hop on!" he said, smiling and pointing to the extra controller.

I took a seat in my gaming chair and pulled the controller into my lap. I could feel his eyes on me.

"I ain't really come to play today. I wanna talk to you about something." I looked up at him as he put his controller down, giving me his undivided attention. "Do you ever think about coming back?"

He sighed. "Son, that's not possible. Necromancy is a myth."

"What if it wasn't?"

"It is!" he answered quickly as irritation oozed from his tone. "Look, son, I'd get nothing out of dreaming of something I know is unattainable. Gabby tried to bring her mom back, and it damn near killed her, so let's just hop on the game and enjoy whatever time we have left of those two hours." He reached for his controller.

"The new coven in town, they're Simone's family. They specialize in spirituality and nature. They said the reason she wasn't able to bring Marie back was because her death wasn't supernatural. They're going to bring Gabby back in a couple of months," I finished, looking up to him.

He cleared his throat. "That's good for them. They didn't really get to have any time together before she was killed."

"That's it?" My eyebrows dropped in confusion. "What about me? Mom?"

"I said no, Nathan!"

I stood abruptly from my chair. "You don't give a fuck about us!"

"Aye, boy." He stood. "You better watch your fuckin' mouth. You big now, but I'll still fuck you up! Now sit your ass down so we can play this game before time runs out."

My jaw flexed. "Nah. I'm good on that. I'll catch you next time," I said before returning to my bedroom in my mom's house as angry tears ran down my cheeks.

CHAPTER 23

GABBY

3 MONTHS LATER:

I JUST FINISHED SHOWERING and was headed down to check Simone's book. There hadn't been any new entries pertaining to Necromancy, but I had a feeling she hadn't ended like I told her to.

I sighed, finding nothing as I ascended the stairs to go warm up leftovers. I'd always had a bad habit of cooking more than I needed, and I was starting to feel more lonely as the days passed. I wanted my family together, and I couldn't help but feel a little envious that Chase was able to experience our daughter and life in a way I never would.

Emerging from my bedroom, I stopped in my tracks to find Chase and a huge Simone standing in the living room. I smiled, approaching them to caress her belly. My granddaughter would be here soon, and I couldn't wait to see her beautiful, tiny face.

"What brings you two by?" I asked as Naomi kicked out against my hand. I loved that name.

"I need to talk to you about something. Well, we do," she replied as I looked up at her before looking over at Chase skeptically.

"Are y'all hungry? I was just about to warm up some leftovers," I answered, quickly turning away to head into the kitchen, trying to calm my nerves. I didn't like the look on either of their faces, which meant I wouldn't like whatever they were here to talk to me about.

Quietly, they took a seat at the table as I prepared the food. The silence was an uncomfortable one. I sat the plates down in front of them before taking my seat in front of mine.

"So?" I finally asked as they continued to stare at me.

I put the forkful of food in my mouth as Simone looked over at Chase before speaking.

"We've been working with Giselle to bring you back, Mommy," she answered shyly in a small voice. My jaw clenched and nostrils flared. Maybe that shit would have worked if she was still a baby. She was hardheaded as fuck. I looked over at Chase. She had to have gotten that shit from him. "Hold up, Mommy. Before you start, daddy told me to let it go, but she told me why it didn't work for you. The death has to be supernatural for any of the spells to work. They're going to help us bring you back."

I sighed, pinching the bridge of my nose. "No!" I answered simply before putting more food into my mouth.

"What?" Simone asked, eyebrows dipped.

"Gabrielle!" Chase started as I lifted a finger to silence him.

"Simone, I already told you what it did to me. I'm not going to let you go through that. You're not sure if it'll work, and you're not taking that risk for me, and that's final."

"I am sure!" She stood and yelled. "We saw it."

I looked over at Chase as he nodded in confirmation. When did her power even manifest into future visions? That didn't matter, though. Those things weren't always accurate. A slight change could change the outcome of any vision. "I said no, Simone. Those visions aren't always set in stone, and Chase knows that. Why didn't you explain that to her?"

"This one is, baby. We saw it together," Chase informed, finally finding his voice again.

I looked back at Simone, whose eyes were teary. "Why don't you wanna come back to us? Don't you want to be there when your granddaughter comes? Why would you miss that when there's a way?" Heavy tears fell onto the table beneath her.

"Why can't you just respect my wishes, Simone? Everything that sounds good isn't. Just because you have new information doesn't mean it's any less dangerous. You're too far along to be taking those types of risks, and what is Nathan saying? He can't be okay with this."

She frowned. "Nathan doesn't have authority over me! It's not his decision, it's mine!"

"But she's his baby too, Simone. That's selfish." I looked over at Chase. "And you're just not gonna say anything? You're the one who roped her into this shit."

"Actually, he didn't. I was researching before he even came back," she said with angry eyes.

"Okay. Let's calm down. Both of you sit," he ordered as we continued our stare down. We were too much alike and very stubborn. "Sit!" he demanded again as we lowered into our seats. "Now, I don't have any input in this back and forth because I'm not on your side with this one, baby."

I looked over at him in disbelief. The nerve of him to go against me in front of her. I could only imagine how much of a shit show it would have been if we were able to raise her like we planned.

"You already know how I feel about this topic, and I've been with her every step of the way. She's going to be okay, and you're going to come home." He reached out to hold my hand. "Close your eyes," he instructed as I obliged.

I gasped as the scene played out underneath my eyelids. There I stood cradling my granddaughter in my arms as Chase stood beside me caressing my back. Simone lay exhausted in the bed. I felt tears running down my cheeks before my eyes opened and landed on a tearful Simone.

I sighed, wiping my eyes, and digging back into my food. It was looking like I wasn't going to win this fight. Was I so wrong for thinking about the wellbeing of my child and hers? Why couldn't they understand where I was coming from? Of course, I wanted to be there for everything, but we were dealt a bad hand.

I could feel their eyes on me, but I couldn't look up. My mind was in turmoil. That vision alone pushed me to agree to their plans, but I couldn't help to revert to my safety concerns. What if the spell knocked her out like it had done me? What if she didn't wake up from it? What if the spell was too much stress on my granddaughter?

"I saw Grandma," she blurted, commanding my attention. "You're the one who told me they have a special connection to the ancestral plain, so you know this will work."

I was still stuck on the first statement. "You... you saw her?"

"Yes, and talked to her, and touched her." I gasped. "She said she had been watching, and she was proud of me. You can see her too when we bring you back."

I looked up at her disobedient ass. "This visit was a courtesy, Mommy. We were going to do it either way, so get ready. You're coming home soon!"

CHAPTER 24

CHASE

I LAY BACK on the couch zoning in and out of the basketball game playing on the TV. Simone had just stopped by to bring me some food from her best friend's restaurant. I was so grateful for our relationship.

My little girl was so beautiful. She resembled her mom so much but with my eyes. Except she wasn't a little girl anymore. She was now a fully grown woman who was having her own little girl. She was so resilient having been through a lot.

Chasity had shown me some memories of when she would check in with her in foster care. I smiled upon seeing her young face but quickly angered due to her living conditions and how she'd been treated. These things could have been avoided had I not shown up that night. Had I not, they wouldn't have been able to track me there. My mom knew how much I loved Gabrielle despite her strong, unnecessary hate toward her.

Then there was Gabrielle. I smiled. Ever since the first day we met, I'd been in love. She was fearless and feisty. By the end of that week, we spent every day together, and I'd known we would be together. She was right, though, about those visions not being definite. Long before I ever proposed to her, I'd seen our future together, and it had been bright. We had plenty of children, and we were happy.

Our demise had never come to me in the form of a vision, which was probably why I didn't hesitate to go after her when she tried to leave. I saw her leaving as an interruption in our future, when all along, it was Cheryl who was the interruption. The way she justified her actions, she was sick!

Checking the time, I headed into my bedroom to get dressed. With my daughter being in my life and pregnant, as well as Gabrielle's soon return. I needed to make sure her prison was still impenetrable. After gathering my things, I jumped to the remote location where Chasity had her imprisoned.

Entering the code, I went in search of Chasity first. Ever since she'd moved our mother in, she hadn't really been to our apartment.

"Chass!" I yelled. She soon came into view. I smiled. I hadn't seen much of my sister since my return, and it was honestly starting to bother me. We were twins, and we'd already spent too long apart from one another as it was.

"Hey, bro, what are you doing here?" she asked, flashing an identical smile. We were damn near one in the same.

"Two reasons. To see you since you haven't been home and pay a little visit to your mom. A lot has happened over the last couple of months and a lot more is going to be happening soon," I responded as she returned a look of confusion. "Simone has been asking about you. When are you coming back?"

"Soon. I just don't want her to try anything if I leave, but what's been happening, and what's about to happen? Is it bad?" she asked, concerned.

I smiled. "No, actually. It's great. There's a new coven in town who happens to be related to Gabrielle and Simone. They're about to try to bring her back." My smile grew wider because she now had one too. She knew how much Gabrielle meant to me. They had also become good friends before everything happened all those years ago. "She ain't too happy about it, though. She didn't want Simone to take the risk, especially being pregnant."

"It can be dangerous, though, Chase. Remember what happened with Gabby. Her reservations are valid."

"She's going to be fine. We have new information we didn't have then. That's why I'm here, though. Where's your mom?" I asked. I'd long ago stopped acknowledging Cheryl as my mom. She'd already taken my fiancée away and had myself or Chasity not shown up, she'd have taken my daughter away, too. She wasn't shit to me but the one who fucked my life up.

"In her cell," she said as I headed in her direction. She sat up on her little cot as soon as I walked in, and a smile spread across her psychotic face. "I was wondering when you were going to come see me. How have you been?" she asked, moving closer to the cell bars.

My jaw clenched. "I'm not here for any pleasantries, Cheryl. You'll rot in here before you see me again. This visit is only a warning. The last one you'll get. My family will be back together soon." Anger and confusion crossed her face. "If so much as a single strand of hair is out of place on my wife, daughter, or granddaughter's head, you'll be dust in the wind."

"Where did I go wrong with you two?"

"Where did your parents go wrong with you? Your coven and your kids hate you. What does that tell you, Cheryl? No one came for you like you thought they would. I control the coven now. There have been, and are going to be, a lot more changes. Your rule as a tyrant is over. You aren't missed, and you never will be!"

She'd crossed more than one line with me, and I didn't give the slightest of a fuck about her anymore. Had there not been pictures, I would have sworn we had no idea why or how my dad had been able to put up with her shit as long as he had.

I turned to head back out and turned back in her direction. "Where's that girl's body?"

Even though I felt the little bitch got what she deserved for trying to get my daughter killed, she also deserved a proper burial from her coven. The dead were important to our covens.

I took slow strides closer to her cell knowingly.

"I'm not telling you anything unless you get me out of here."

I quickly stuck my hands between the cell bars and gripped her temples, closing my eyes to search her memories for what I needed.

After minutes of searching, I let go and stepped back. "You're sick as fuck," I exclaimed before leaving. I found Chasity down in the kitchen area. "When are you coming back home?" I inquired again. I missed my sister... my twin, and our connection.

"I'll visit soon, but I don't want to leave for days at a time until I'm sure there's no way for her to escape."

"If you'd just kill her, you wouldn't have to worry about any of that." I was sick of this shit. She'd been putting this off for years. I wanted to do it before Simone was born, but I let Chasity talk me out of it, and look where it's gotten me.

She ignored me, moving around the kitchen. "When are you going to be doing the ceremony?"

"Couple days. The coven's been getting settled in, and Simone's supposed to be resting, but she's just as hardheaded and stubborn as her mom." I shook my head.

She smiled. "When's the baby due?"

"Next month."

"I'm happy for you, bro. You still get to have a relationship with your daughter, despite everything, and see your granddaughter grow up." She sighed. "Simone is capable of a lot more than she knows. She's going to be very powerful once she reaches her full potential, and there are going to be others after her, Chase. Mom isn't the only threat to her."

"And they'll suffer the same fate as your mom will if anything ever happens to any of them. You won't be able to protect her, Chas. I don't even know why you try. She isn't worth it."

"She's still our mom, Chase."

I wasn't about to keep wasting my breath on this pointless conversation. I kissed her forehead and embraced her tightly.

"I'll see you later, Chas. I love you!" I said before jumping back to our shared apartment.

CHAPTER 25

SIMONE

Nathan had been moping around the past couple of days because he couldn't have his way and stop me from being a part of tonight's ceremony. I didn't care what he thought, I was bringing my mom back today.

He'd been acting a bit off for a couple of months, and whenever I tried to hear his thoughts, he blocked me out. I stood in the kitchen, eyeing him as he sat in front the TV flicking through the same channels repeatedly. He hadn't even really been playing his game, which was not like him at all.

I walked over and eased into his lap, and his hands instantly went to my stomach. I left multiple kisses on his soft lips.

"Baby, what's on your mind? I can tell something's bothering you. Talk to me." I ran my fingers through his soft curls. "Please. You're being distant, and I don't like that."

"I'm sorry, baby," he stated simply, looking down as he continued to caress my belly.

I cupped his face so he could look up at me. "Why are you blocking me out, baby?"

"I went to talk to my dad about possibly bringing him back, too, and in so many words he said no. My mom had already warned me he'd say no. That's it, baby. Nothing serious. I just been thinking a lot." I caressed the side of his face. He rarely, if ever, got like this, so I knew this had to have really been bothering him. "She said all those memories of how he was killed would come back with him. I get it, though. I was just mad because he didn't even give it a thought."

"Have you been back to see him since?" I asked knowingly.

"No, and that was a couple of months ago." I

turned his head toward me and pecked his lips before pulling him into a tight hug.

"Go see your dad, bae," I ordered before standing from his lap and heading upstairs to get dressed.

I sat on the edge of my bed, putting on my shoes, when I felt a presence. Looking over, I saw Nayeli's feline standing in the doorway staring before stepping inside.

Are you sure about tonight? She asked telepathically. I nodded and continued to get dressed.

The further along she got in her pregnancy, the harder it had been for her to complete her transformations. She would be accompanying me to the ceremony tonight. She was equally as worried as Nathan. I didn't understand why they just couldn't trust that I knew I was making the right decision.

I'm a little nervous, Simone. Is Nathan coming?

"Don't be nervous, and I doubt it. We're going to be fine. Just trust me." I stood before leaving the room and heading downstairs as Nayeli followed close behind. I entered the living room to find Nathan and Jessie on the couch, fully engrossed in the game. "Aight, baby, we are about to head out. Give me a kiss," I demanded, turning his face toward me. I pecked his soft lips a couple of times. "Don't forget to go see your dad, bae," I finished, staring down at him as he nodded. Nayeli jumped down from Jessie's lap, and we left.

After a thirty minute drive, we were driving through the wooded area leading to Africa town. They had already made so many much-needed changes in the short time they'd been living there. They planted gardens all over as well as flowers. They fixed up a lot of the worn homes in the small community as well as starting to build their own permanent homes on the vacant land. They revamped the park for the kids. The only place that didn't need to be revamped was the cemetery. It had been the only area that was kept up after all these years.

I stopped my car on the curb of my grandma's house before getting out and wobbling up the sidewalk then the stairs. Damn near out of breath, I pulled the screen door open to find the twins sitting on the living room floor watching TV. I greeted them and headed to the kitchen to find Giselle cleaning fresh vegetables as she swayed to the Caribbean music playing aloud. She looked up at me smiling as Nayeli jumped onto the barstool.

"Hello, ladies!" she said before turning into the fridge. "Are you ready for the ceremony? Some of the coven members are over in the cemetery setting up." She looked off to the side before smiling. "Marie says hello as well. She's excited about tonight."

"Hey, Grandma!" I said aloud, smiling. "Yes. More than ready."

I didn't know exactly where she was in the room since I couldn't see her unless Giselle and I were holding hands. I couldn't wait to be able to hug my mom on this side and for them to be able to see each other after all these years. After tonight's ceremony, I'd happily sit my ass down for the remainder of this pregnancy. Not like I really had a choice. I'd gotten away with it for so long because Nathan had been pushing the issue alone. After tonight, he'd have extra reinforcements.

I went over to make myself comfortable on the couch to calm the little nerves I did have. Of course, I was nervous, but I couldn't say it aloud. They'd definitely try to postpone the ceremony, but I didn't want to wait another day, let alone the rest of my pregnancy.

"We're about ready to head over," Giselle informed as she entered the living room, and the twins stood.

We all followed her out the front door before she halted on the porch as numerous headlights could be seen coming down the street. My features softened when I saw Eva and Tally in the first car. "It's okay. That's our coven."

Tally parked on the curb in front of Nathan's grandma's house before getting out.

"We came to help however we can," she informed us as the street quickly filled with at least twenty of my coven members.

I smiled as we took the short five-minute walk to the cemetery. The support was overwhelming. My mom had to have some impact to have people behind her twenty-one years after her death.

As soon as we walked up to the entrance, my dad came into view. I smiled again as he pulled me into a tight hug. He hadn't really expressed it, but I knew that he had some reservations about me being here and participating, but there was no way I was missing this.

There were crystals, stones, and candles circling my mother's grave as the crowd gathered around as well. There were ancient symbols painted on her headstone. We all joined hands. My dad and Tally were on either side of me as Nayeli snuggled close to my leg. Giselle stood center holding a worn spell book opened to marked pages.

Suddenly, I felt arms around me and looked to the side to see Nathan. He kissed my neck. "I wasn't gonna miss this, baby."

I blushed, turning back to Giselle as she started the chant, and the Gullah witches joined in before the Africa town coven did as well.

A strong gust of wind whipped through the circle as the candles threatened to go out. I looked up to see flashes of spirits floating above the circle, only being able to make out my grandma's face.

A large portal opened beside Giselle as the chant continued and intensified. I looked through and could see the living room from the cabin. I gripped my locket tighter, calling out to her with my eyes closed tightly.

Gasps and more intense chanting caused my lids to pop back open to find the portal getting smaller as they attempted to keep it opened. I looked around to everyone straining to keep the portal open as long as they could, and she still hadn't come through.

I reached down to make sure the bracelet was secure around my wrist and gripped the charm on my necklace. Nathan's grip had loosened, and I took that opportunity to bolt from his arms.

"No! Simone," he yelled right before I jumped through.

What the fuck did we just do that for? Nayeli asked telepathically as I looked down at her feline form. I didn't think she'd jump through with me.

"What are you doing, Nayeli? Go back!" I replied before heading into the bedroom. "Ma!" I yelled again before the secret door slid open, and she appeared.

"Simone, what are you doing here?" she asked after looking down at Nayeli confused. "How did she—" She stopped herself, looking around me at the dwindling portal. "Simone, what did you do? How are y'all here, and what is that?"

I sighed at all those questions before gripping her arm and pulling her out. "Come on!"

She ain't have to bring shit with her. It should all already be in the real cabin. Nayeli jumped through first, and I was right behind her with a tight grip on my mom's wrist.

The portal had gotten smaller and had to turn to pull her through as Nathan and my dad also broke the circle to assist. As soon as she came through, the portal quickly closed, and the candles had gone out.

Tally waved a single finger, and a bright light shone down over all of us. My mom stood in place looking down at her hands as everybody gasped, watching her transform before our eyes. Her hair stretched a couple of inches further down her back. Her face widened a bit, and a couple extra pounds appeared around her arms, legs, and waist. She looked up at me smiling, and at her correct age, she didn't look much different than before.

She reached out and quickly pulled me into a tight hug as I sobbed like this had been my first time seeing her. It had really worked. I wouldn't have admitted it, but I too had my reservations about its success. Giselle had made it seem too simple after all my research made it seem damn near impossible.

She kissed the top of my head and pulled away to look down at me as she wiped my tears away. She looked up at my dad, who wore the same smile as us. I stepped aside as Nathan quickly pulled me back into his arms.

"You ain't gone be satisfied until I fuck you up, Simone," he whispered the threat into my ear as I enjoyed the scene before me. I knew I'd be in for the world's longest tongue lashing from him, but I knew how to make him forget about it. I lay my head back into his chest as I continued to enjoy the scene. Suddenly, my eyelids got heavy.

"Simone?" my mom inquired. Her stepping around my dad was the last thing I heard before I collapsed into Nathan, and everything went black.

CHAPTER 26

CAMERON

MONTHS HAD GONE BY, and I still rarely left my apartment and had no contact outside of it, not even with my parents. They'd been calling and leaving messages. The last one threatened to pop up if I didn't visit, so I was headed home today for a visit.

I'm pretty sure he didn't know, but whatever Nathan had tried to do to me didn't work. I knew I should have followed my first mind when he knocked on my door. I should have never let him in knowing Nayeli and Simone were thick as thieves. I was still so confused at what was even happening. I hadn't been doing anything but sulking and playing the game.

I had never been so alone in my damn life. I sometimes still missed Nayeli. I really loved that girl and thought we were gonna be together, but she had some other shit going on with her. I was feeling like I had just gotten out of that relationship right on time.

I finished my last game of Fortnite and went into my bedroom to finish packing. I didn't plan to stay long, but maybe this was what I needed. To get away. I tossed my duffle over my shoulder and gripped my baseball bat tightly as I peered out of the peephole before exiting and checking my surroundings. My head remained on a swivel as I hightailed it to my car and pulled out.

The four-hour drive home to Savannah, Georgia was peaceful. The more space I put in between myself and everything having to do with Alabama, the more at peace I was feeling. Before I knew it, I was pulling into my parents' long driveway and parking in the circle.

As soon as I stepped out to grab my duffle from the back, my mom was descending the stairs with the biggest smile, causing me to do the same. She pulled me into a tight hug.

"My baby," she said, pulling away to leave kisses all over my face. "I missed you so much. I wish you'd just move back home." I rolled my eyes. If it'd been up to them, I'd never have left and would still be living in my childhood bedroom. "Come on. I made lunch, and your dad is inside waiting for us."

I sighed as I followed her inside. I was already annoyed and hadn't even started on the earful I was about to receive from my dad. I dropped my bag in the living room and went to wash my hands before heading into the kitchen. My dad's angry eyes immediately landed on me and followed me all the way to my seat. Nigga wasn't as intimidating as he thought he was. Hell, I was more afraid of Nayeli than his ass. We ate in silence for a while but knew it wouldn't last long.

"You tell your mom why you had her up here worried sick about your ass yet?" he asked, never looking away from his food.

I sat in silence as I continued to eat. I hadn't come up with a lie yet, but there was no way I'd even attempt to try telling them the truth. Nobody would believe that outlandish ass story. He cleared his throat as we made eye contact.

"I've been having a lot going on," I answered simply before stuffing food into my mouth.

My mom frowned. "Like what? How have you and Nayeli been?"

I stared back at her for a minute. "We broke up a while ago."

Her frown deepened. She loved her. They loved us together.

Fuck it, I thought before deciding to go for it and tell them everything. I avoided their gazes as I continued to tear into my food. I'd missed my mama's cooking too, especially because I didn't have Nayeli's anymore.

After minutes of silence, I finally looked up. They'd probably try to have me committed now.

"I told you we shouldn't have let him go to school out there," my mom snapped at my dad as she teared up.

He sighed. "I thought we cleared that area," he started as I frowned. "What else did they do to you, son?" he asked, placing his fork down giving me his undivided attention.

I frowned. "Wait, you believe me?"

"It's time to tell him the truth about what it is we do, honey," my mom said to him. What did she mean by that? For as long as I could remember, my parents ran their own private investigation firm, and it brought in great money. I never wanted for shit growing up, and we always lived in this big ass house. She stood and prompted me to follow her. My dad stood as well, following close behind me.

Walking into my dad's home office, my mom opened the middle drawer of his desk and pressed a button before the bookshelf slid open. I stared between the two of them before she motioned for me to enter.

I walked slowly down the dimly lit corridor before coming out to what looked to be an arsenal, among other things. Any handgun or machine gun you could think of graced the length of the wall. Cases of dart bullets. Shelves of vials filled with different color liquids. A computer monitor embedded into the countertop with red dots blinking in sporadic areas over the map of the United States.

I turned to them. Who the fuck were they? Whatever this was they'd done a great job hiding it because I didn't have the slightest clue of all this being here.

"The PI firm is a front for what your mom and I actually do for a living," my dad finally spoke.

"Which is?"

My mom walked over to the vials, sifting through them until she found the one she'd been looking for. "Witch hunters," she answered, turning back in my direction and holding the vial out to me. "This will lift any magic that has ever been used on you."

I looked between the two of them again.

"You're kidding, right? There's no such thing," I answered, amused as their expressions remained the same. My smirk dropped. That wasn't so far-fetched, given what Nayeli and Nathan had done to me.

She ran her thumb across the charm on my chain. "Last time you were home to visit I had a bad feeling. This amulet is the reason the memory wipe spell didn't work," she stated as I looked down at it.

I'd never really given it a thought. She'd just given it to me and told me to never take it off. I just figured it was another expensive gift. Popping the top off the vial, I downed the orange liquid. Coughing hysterically, I gripped the edges of the counter to keep my balance.

I hovered the counter catching my breath. Suddenly, my eyes rolled backward as foreign memories invaded my head. I saw Nayeli and Simone, but mostly Nathan, in different situations doing crazy unexplainable shit.

My eyes returned to normal as I continued to gasp for air holding onto the counter. After catching my breath, I looked up at my parents who waited with concerned expressions.

"Are you okay? What did you see, baby?" my mom asked, nearing me.

I shook my head in disbelief. "She tried to tell me that Simone was a witch, and she is her familiar. She takes on different cat forms." They shared a look. "I didn't take it well at all, and she cried hysterically, so Nathan wiped my memory." I leaned backward in shock. I couldn't believe any of this shit.

She'd tried to tell me about everything, and I spazzed on her. She looked hurt. She didn't want to break up, she literally had to. She did love a nigga, and she really wasn't cheating. I smiled a little before it quickly faded.

My dad sighed, leaning back against the doorway before looking over at my mom. "We'll take care of it."

To be continued...